He leaned in closer as he flattened his palms on either side of her head.

It would be so easy to turn this into something more, right here and now.

They were alone. There was nothing stopping him. And he knew Annabelle was his for the taking.

Colt shifted until his lips grazed across hers like a whisper. "A man could get used to hearing a beautiful woman give him compliments."

"Then maybe you should find a beautiful woman who wants to," she murmured.

He nipped at her bottom lip. "I've found her."

"Colt." Her hands came up to his chest.

How could he want someone so desperately? He had always been able to control his needs, but not with Annabelle. She challenged him in so many ways, and she was the one woman he really shouldn't want.

Still, seducing her was too sweet, too perfect.

Keeping one hand beside her face, he ran the other over her hip. His thumb slid beneath the hem of her tank. Her smooth skin beneath his touch was everything he'd been dreaming of...and he'd dreamed of her plenty last night.

"I want you," he said.

"No, you want to control me."

"Only in bed."

* * *

Twin Secrets is part of The Rancher's Heirs series—

Loyalty and family mean everything to these Texas men and the women who tame them.

Dear Reader,

Welcome to the first installment of my brand-new series featuring hunky cowboys and adorable babies! I am so excited to introduce you to the world of Pebblebrook Ranch. These four brothers are quite different, yet completely swoonworthy!

First up is Colt, the youngest of the Elliott boys and a twin. I had such a great time discovering these characters. The banter was fun to write and this story is quite possibly one of my favorites. (Can I say that?)

Seriously, there is something so magical when the stories just present themselves to me and that's precisely what happened with *Twin Secrets*. My mind was going faster than I could type. These characters definitely knew what they wanted and I had no choice but to go along for the ride!

I do hope you enjoy the first book in this series and anticipate stories from the other sexy, mysterious Elliott brothers: Nolan, Hayes and Beau.

Happy Reading!

Jules

JULES BENNETT

—

TWIN SECRETS

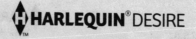

Recycling programs
for this product may
not exist in your area.

ISBN-13: 978-0-373-83833-2

Twin Secrets

Printed in U.S.A.

National bestselling author **Jules Bennett** has penned over forty contemporary romance novels. She lives in the Midwest with her high-school-sweetheart husband and their two kids. Jules can often be found on Twitter chatting with readers, and you can also connect with her via her website, julesbennett.com.

Books by Jules Bennett

Harlequin Desire

What the Prince Wants
A Royal Amnesia Scandal
Maid for a Magnate
His Secret Baby Bombshell

Mafia Moguls

Trapped with the Tycoon
From Friend to Fake Fiancé
Holiday Baby Scandal
The Heir's Unexpected Baby

The Rancher's Heirs

Twin Secrets

Harlequin Special Edition

The St. Johns of Stonerock

Dr. Daddy's Perfect Christmas
The Fireman's Ready-Made Family
From Best Friend to Bride

Visit her Author Profile page at Harlequin.com, or julesbennett.com, for more titles.

This goes to Stacy Boyd, who said she loves cowboys and baby stories...so I delivered an entire series of both! Thanks for the ideas!

One

How the hell could her father have gambled away all of his savings? As in, every last penny to his name. His reckless way of living finally caught up with him…with them. He'd lost major things before: his car, his retirement funds, all of her mother's jewelry—save for the one piece Annabelle had hidden away. But he'd gone too far this time.

As if Annabelle Carter didn't have enough on her plate. She'd come home to Stone River, Texas, to start over. She'd brought her sweet twins, six-month-old Emily and Lucy, and planned to offer them a new life and begin building her dream…a vision of her late mother's.

But, no. Now Annabelle was driving to the ranch next door to do damage control. As she turned onto the

long drive, flanked by a pristine white fence, she pulled
in a breath. The arched, metal sign over the entrance
was a good indicator of the amount of money these
people had. The stone columns suspending the sign
were nothing short of remarkable. The beauty started
from the street and she could only imagine what she
was about to see at the end of this drive.

Pebblebrook Ranch was one place she'd never ventured into. It was owned by the hoity-toity Elliott family, and they didn't necessarily run in the same circles.
The five–thousand-acre spread boasted several massive
homes. Just one of their mansions was worth more than
Annabelle's entire farm.

And that was when they'd actually had livestock.
Her father, however, had gambled animals away, too.
She'd been gone two years, living in Houston, and in
that time he'd completely lost everything.

Rage ripped through her. What would he have done
had she not come back home to nurse her own wounds?
A fresh wave of anger surged through Annabelle as she
remembered her sister and fiancé's betrayal. And the
crippling effects of her sister's recent death. So much
pain, Annabelle wasn't sure how to log it all inside her
heart.

Now she had to deal with Colt Elliott on top of everything else. She'd never met the man, but she knew
of the Elliott brothers. Sexy ladies' men, all much older
than her. If she recalled correctly, Colt was a twin. Were
the twins the youngest of the siblings?

None of that mattered. What mattered was that her
father had borrowed money to pay off the farm loan be-

fore it could go into foreclosure, without informing her. Of all people to go to, her father had gone to Colt Elliott. Not that there were many people who could've helped, but Neil Carter could have come to Annabelle first. She didn't have that chunk of cash, but she would've gone through hell before borrowing from the Elliotts.

Now her father owed Colt instead of the bank. Perfect. Just perfect. The loan had been so close to being paid off, but her father just couldn't hang on any longer. He'd gone through all the money he'd put aside. Thankfully, Annabelle had set aside money for her sister's funeral expenses, or her father would've gone through that, as well.

According to her father, he and Colt had come to an agreement that he had to pay off the debt within three months. The bimonthly payments couldn't be a day late or a penny short or the farm would permanently belong to Colt.

Fine. Annabelle had no problem taking over her dad's end of the bargain. She refused to lose the only thing she had left. Her childhood home would not go to the family whose hobby was probably sitting around counting their wad of cash.

Annabelle's father claimed Colt was helping, but she didn't believe that for a second. People like the Elliotts didn't just do things out of the kindness of their hearts. In terms of wealth and influence, they were a giant leap above all other people in this town. With their mansions on the sprawling estate, the billions of dollars that passed through the farm from all their livestock… the rest of the businesses in the area didn't even com-

pare. They were Stone River's answer to a cattle mo-
nopoly…if that was a thing. Random people didn't just
go to Pebblebrook. It was like some sacred ground that
mere peons didn't dare trespass on.

Well, too bad because she wanted to know what
Colt's agenda truly was. She suspected he wanted her
land for himself and she was going to have no part of
that. She had her own dreams: marriage, siblings for
her twins, opening her bed-and-breakfast. She'd already
lost so much—she wasn't about to lose her home or
her future.

Annabelle approached the sprawling three-story
log and stone home. Sturdy wooden porches stretched
across the first and second floors and two balconies
extended from double glass doors off the third floor.
Probably bedrooms. She imagined Colt on a balcony
overlooking his massive estate, as if he were a king
overlooking his kingdom. Annabelle swallowed. She
couldn't even fathom the money these people had.

When a horse came from around the side of the two-
story stable, Annabelle immediately forgot about the
house. And it wasn't even the striking black stallion
that had her attention.

Hellllo, Shirtless Stable Boy.

She may be nursing a shattered heart but she wasn't
dead, and this hottie with excellent, tanned muscle tone
was a perfect temporary distraction. How much work
did it take to get ripped like that? Ranching certainly
produced some fine—

Annabelle jerked as her car hit something and came
to an abrupt stop. Gripping the wheel, eyes squeezed

shut, she had no clue what had just happened, but she'd been distracted and obviously ran into...*oh, please don't be a person or an animal.*

Opening one eye at a time, she saw nothing but the barn and grassy fields...and the shattered post where the fence had been. Mercy, she'd been so caught up in the hunk on horseback, she'd run into the fence. Way to make an entrance.

As if she needed another problem in her life.

Mortified and shaken up, Annabelle shut off her car, thankful the babies weren't in the backseat. Her door jerked open, startling a squeal out of her.

"Are you all right, ma'am?"

That perfect Southern drawl combined with the bare chest she now stared at was enough to render her speechless. But even that couldn't override the reason she came. Just because she'd wrecked her sporty car, her only material possession worth any money, didn't mean she could deviate from her plan. What was one more setback at this point?

"I'm fine," she stated, trembling more from the sight of the sexy stranger than the actual accident.

Annabelle swung her legs out and came to stand, but the cowboy didn't back up. With one hand on her open car door and the other on the hood, he had her trapped. On any other day, she would've welcomed this stranger getting in her space and making her forget her cheating fiancé, but today there was no time for lustful thoughts. She shivered again as his eyes swept over her.

"Sorry about the fence," she stated, shoving her hair away from her face. "I'll pay to have it repaired."

With the savings that were supposed to go toward realizing my mother's dream.

"The sun was in my eyes," she went on. No way was she about to admit she'd been staring at his perfect... riding form.

"Don't worry about the fence."

Now he stepped back, but just enough for her to take in his well-worn cowboy boots, fitted jeans over a narrow waist...that glistening chest and his tipped cowboy hat. Black, of course.

"What brings you to Pebblebrook?" he asked, propping his hands on his hips.

Annabelle pulled in a breath. "I'm here to see Mr. Elliott. My name is Annabelle Carter and I live next door. Well, I used to a few years ago, but I'm back now."

Despite the chiseled jaw and the heavy-lidded gaze, the man's mouth tipped into a slight grin. "Well, ma'am, Mr. Elliott is busy right now. Is there something I can help you with? A glass of sweet tea? You look like you could use a break."

Sharing a sweet tea, or anything else with this hunky stranger, was tempting, but not on her agenda.

Annabelle blew out a breath. Mr. Elliott was busy. Of course. Probably at the bank purchasing more properties to add to his collection. A man like Colt didn't work outside in the heat tending to his own animals and land. That would be too far beneath him.

"You work here?" she asked, crossing her arms.

His mouth twitched again. "Yes, ma'am."

"Then give your boss a message." She may not be able to talk to the man himself, but she would leave her mark—and she didn't mean the broken fence. "I'd like to talk to him about my ranch next door and the agreement he made with my father. Please tell Mr. Elliott, when he's done getting his manicure or finished stealing puppies from children, he will be dealing with me from now on. I'll be waiting at my house for his visit."

Because she certainly wouldn't be showing her face here again.

The stable hand simply tapped the brim of his black hat and tipped his head. "I'll be sure to let him know."

His eyes raked over her once more, sending shivers through her despite the Texas heat. "Are you sure you don't want something to drink? Have a seat on the porch. You look like you could use a break."

Oh, she could use a break. Like a monthlong vacation somewhere exotic with a fruity umbrella drink full of alcohol and unlimited refills. But she'd just settle for a break from all the pain life kept dishing out.

"No, I don't have the time." Not to mention, she couldn't stay in his presence too much longer. It was difficult keeping her eyes off that broad chest sprinkled with dark hair and the tattoo on his right bicep.

"Is there anything else I should pass on?" he asked.

Since she was in a mood, she nodded. "I'm not a pushover like my father. Make sure you tell him he has twenty-four hours to contact me."

The "or else" hung in the air, but she had no idea what her "or else" threat would be so she left it at that. She hoped she sounded badass, but it was kind of hard with her bright red car mounting the fence.

The cowboy stepped toward the front of her vehicle,

assessing the damage. She didn't even want to know how this would affect her insurance. *One crisis at a time.*

"Your little car has quite a bit of damage, ma'am."

With a flick of his fingertip, he adjusted his hat, bringing that cobalt blue gaze up to hers. The striking color of his eyes only added to his appeal. Did all the stable hands at this ranch have the qualifications to do calendars? Because she wouldn't mind buying one of those.

"I'm pretty sure this would fit in the bed of my truck," he muttered around a grin. "Should I haul it next door for you?"

Annabelle ignored his snarky jab. It was only because of his sex appeal that she let the question slide. Besides, she wasn't here to impress people or make friends.

"I can drive. Thank you."

She turned to get back into her car. As she started it up again, the cowboy closed her door, then leaned inside the window. "I'll be sure Mr. Elliott gets in touch with you today."

Annabelle nodded and shifted into gear. He stepped back, giving her one last glimpse of the fine body she didn't have time to fully appreciate.

Disappointed that she hadn't gotten face time with Colt Elliott, Annabelle headed back down the drive and prepared the speech she'd deliver when she did see him. She was done letting life—and men—rob her of her dreams.

* * *

He watched her tiny red car until it disappeared at the end of the drive. Annabelle Carter was one fired-up woman. The vibrant red hair and flashing green eyes had him more intrigued than he should be.

When he'd come around the side of the barn to put Lightning away after his morning ride, he'd caught a glimpse of the car just before it missed the turn in the drive and slammed into the fence.

"Colt?"

He turned to see Josh, one of his best stable hands, heading his way.

"Everything all right?" he asked. At nearly forty, Josh was probably Colt's hardest worker.

Colt nodded toward the fence. "This is top priority. Tell Ryan to assist you. I'll put Lightning in her stall."

Colt almost wished he hadn't fired a worker last week, but the guy had it coming and Colt didn't put up with lazy. He worked too damn hard. Just because his bank account had more zeroes than this town had ever seen, didn't mean he wasn't a hands-on type of guy— in business and in pleasure.

Josh nodded. "Is the lady okay?"

Speaking of hands-on...

Was she? Colt thought of the way she'd demanded to see "Mr. Elliott." He nearly lost it when she mentioned a manicure and puppy stealing. She truly didn't have a high opinion of him, but that was fine. He'd seen the sexual interest when he'd gotten close. She was pretty damn sexy herself.

But Colt hadn't been ready to tell her who he was

until he knew what she wanted. Being mistaken for a worker was just one of the advantages of loving the ranch life. He may be the owner, well, he and his three brothers, but Colt was by far the most active. He took pride in what he had. There was no question of authority around here and his staff respected him. He wouldn't have it any other way.

Keeping in control of every situation is what led him to the success he had today. So, letting Annabelle believe he was just a ranch hand had definitely worked to his advantage. Now he had time to plot, to think of exactly how he wanted to play this situation out.

She said she was back in town, and he hadn't missed the way she'd looked at his chest. Maybe a little flirting, even a little seduction, would be in order.

Colt mounted Lightning and trotted back to the stable while Josh went to get supplies to fix the broken fence. Annabelle may be more financially savvy than her old man, but that wouldn't change the outcome.

The documents Neil Carter had signed without taking the time to read were completely legal and binding.

Colt had been wanting to get that land for years. The Carter's five-hundred-acre farm wasn't vast in comparison to his, but he and his brothers had shared a vision of owning it. Their main goal was to turn the property into an adjoining dude ranch. The Carter home was perfect for additional housing for guests.

Colt's father had always been a dreamer, not a doer. He'd discussed owning a dude ranch, having people come to stay on their property and learn the ways of their life, but he'd never gotten beyond the talking stage.

Dementia had stolen Grant Elliott's mind, leaving Colt to carry on and bring his father's legacy to life.

From the time Colt was a young boy, he'd itched to see this property grow, to see people from all over flock in and see what they'd created. He refused to let anything stand in the way of his goal, even the sassy, beautiful Ms. Carter.

After putting the saddle and blanket away, he grabbed the brush to groom the dust from Lightning. While stroking the stallion, an epiphany struck him. Colt was a smarter businessman than Neil, clearly. Hell, Colt knew Neil had no idea what he'd agreed to when he'd accepted the money to pay off the loan—the man had been too desperate. But Colt would give Annabelle a chance to pay that debt. There were six installments left. Three months was all that stood between him and everything he'd ever wanted.

Suddenly being one stable hand short wasn't such a hardship. Perhaps Annabelle would be interested in a little work to help pay off the debt. She no doubt wanted to discuss the arrangement. She'd controlled her anger with him, thinking she'd just been talking to a stable hand, but there had been fury in those deep green eyes. Well, he'd use that fury to his advantage and make her an offer she couldn't refuse.

Colt patted the side of the stallion and finished brushing him as his brilliant plan took shape. He had no intention of ever handing that land over again. It finally belonged to him, but her father had to learn a lesson. He owed more than just this debt, but Annabelle didn't need to know that.

Having such a beautiful woman on his property sure would perk things up around here. She had drive and determination. He couldn't help but admire her spirit.

Colt whistled as he headed back toward the main house. His limp from the accident wasn't even bothering him today. Sometimes it ached, but right now, he had his mind on other things…like the sexy redhead he needed to properly introduce himself to.

He made his way to his third-floor master suite to get ready for a very important meeting. He owned the land, now he wanted to own the woman. And Colt Elliott always got what he wanted.

Two

Infuriating man.

Annabelle found herself on Colt Elliott's property for the second time today. She'd wanted to have the meeting in her house, where she could have some level of control. But when Colt's assistant or minion, or whatever, had called, he'd made it clear that Colt would meet with her, and only her, at precisely 7:00 p.m. at Pebblebrook. Otherwise, the meeting was off.

Damn infuriating man. She'd never met him and she already despised the air he breathed.

Whatever. She just wanted this to be over with. The sooner she could get Colt to agree to her terms, the better. Hopefully he'd see that this new arrangement would be beneficial to both of them. No matter what he threw at her, Annabelle wasn't leaving until she had something to cling to, some hope that she wasn't doomed to a life of failure when she was only twenty-four years old.

She was a mother to two beautiful twin girls now. Her father was doting all over them at the moment and would have to be her babysitter when she found a job. He was responsible with children, just not money. Besides, she couldn't afford to pay a sitter for one kid, let alone two.

First, she had to get this debt straightened out, and then she'd focus on getting that job. Surely, there was something in town she could do. At this point, she wasn't going to be picky.

Smoothing her hands down her green sundress, she pulled in a deep breath. Her nerves weren't about to abate, so she rang the bell and stepped back...waiting to enter the enemy's lair.

This place was so huge, it was almost intimidating. A wooden bridge arched slightly over a creek that ran in front of the house between the drive and the entrance.

The man literally sat in his castle, complete with moat, waiting on the town peons to enter his kingdom. Oh, how she wished someone would knock him down a peg or two. She had an unhealthy dose of anger stored up with Colt Elliott's name written all over it.

She wasn't even getting into the anger she had toward her father for putting her in this position to begin with. All he'd told her is that Colt had fronted the money and the loan was paid off. Now they owed Colt, not the bank. She made sure her father got that in writing from Colt and Neil had said he did sign a paper and it had been notarized. So, at least her father had been smart enough not to just do things the old-fashioned way with a handshake and a promise. Because Annabelle didn't trust Colt Elliott. Not one iota.

The double doors swung open and an elderly man stood before her. Annabelle thought the Elliott boys' father had passed some years ago, so she wasn't sure who this man was.

"Come in, Ms. Carter. Mr. Elliott is expecting you."

She stepped over the threshold and nearly gasped. If she'd thought the outside was spectacular, the inside was breathtaking.

The entryway allowed her to see all the way up to the third story. An open walkway on both floors connected each side of the house, allowing anyone upstairs to see the entire foyer.

Annabelle was getting a vibe that Colt liked to look down on people, to belittle them. Well, he may have pushed her father around, but he was about to deal with a whole new game player. She wanted to know precisely why he'd extended his hand of generosity to her family. Nobody did something like this just to play nice.

"I'm Charlie." The older gentleman closed the door and tipped his head down in greeting. "If you'll follow me, I'll take you to Mr. Elliott."

Annabelle continued taking in all the beauty of this home, and tried not to let jealousy take over. The Elliotts existed on a whole other level than her family ever had, especially now that they had nothing. But Annabelle wasn't about to let life run her over. She'd had enough and Colt Elliott was about to get the brunt of her frustrations.

The calming trickle of water drew her attention as she passed by a sunken living area. Who the hell had a waterfall wall in their home? Oh, right. The people who counted their billions as a hobby.

Annabelle forced her frustrations aside and continued on behind Charlie. There was a bigger issue at hand. She wasn't going to spend her time assessing how this family lived so lavishly when everything had been robbed from hers. Everyone created their own destiny; unfortunately, she was the victim of her father's.

No more. Annabelle had a vision for her future and it certainly didn't involve giving up her childhood home. Once she got to the bottom of this ordeal, she could start on rebuilding her life. Because she wasn't just worried about herself anymore, there were two sweet babies to consider.

Charlie led her through a maze and she wondered if she'd ever find her way out once this meeting was over. Finally, he stopped in front of an oversize arched doorway. He tapped his knuckles on the door before easing it open.

"Sir, Ms. Carter is here."

Nerves gathered heavily in her belly as she smoothed her sundress down one last time. She didn't care what her emotions were, and there were plenty, but she had to keep them hidden. Someone like Colt Elliott would home in on any weakness and use it to his advantage. Clearly, or she wouldn't be here trying to get her house back from the man who'd snatched it from her father during one of his worst moments.

Charlie eased the door open and stepped back with

a nod before disappearing back down the labyrinth of hallways.

Shoulders back, ready to battle the enemy, Annabelle stepped into the spacious office complete with a wall of windows overlooking back acreage. The second she shifted her focus to the other end of the room, she stilled. Her heart clenched, breath caught in her throat.

"You," she gritted through her teeth. If it wasn't Shirtless Stable Boy himself.

Colt had been right. She was just as stunning as he remembered. He wondered if he'd still feel the same way once he'd had time to process the events of earlier. But now that Annabelle Carter was in his home, he took another moment to appreciate the entire package.

That vibrant red hair, wide green eyes, simple makeup and a green dress that she probably thought practical...he found it tempting. How long would it take to undo each of those tiny buttons down the front?

"You lied," she accused him, not moving any farther into the room.

Colt rose from behind the antique desk that had belonged to his father, and his father before him. He circled it and came to lean against the front. Crossing his ankles, he rested his hands on either side of his hips and shrugged. He always appreciated a good sparring opponent.

"I didn't lie," he amended. "I told you Mr. Elliott was busy when you asked. And I was. I had just finished exercising my stallion and needed to get him brushed and fed. I wasn't getting a manicure or stealing puppies. I save those fun events for Saturdays."

Her expressive green eyes narrowed as she slowly made her way across the room. Oh, she was going to be so fun. He didn't miss the way she took her time in assessing him, as well. Let her look. If all went as planned, she'd have plenty of opportunities to do more than caress him with her eyes.

"What is it you wanted to see me about?" he asked, ready to hear what she thought she could do to rectify this situation. He had a plan of his own to throw at her.

"I hardly recognize you with your shirt on."

So, Ms. Annabelle had claws. He liked that in a woman, preferably when she clawed at his back, but verbally would do…for now.

Colt couldn't hide his smile. She was definitely going to be more of a joy to deal with than Neil Carter.

"If you're requesting I take it off, I'm happy to oblige."

She crossed her arms over her chest, doing nothing to deter him from appreciating her lush shape. "The only thing you can oblige me with is discussing the terms of this contract you have with my father."

"Not my first choice during a meeting with a beautiful woman." Colt stood straight up, ready to get down to business. Obviously, they would have to get this out of the way first. "The arrangement is simple, as I'm sure he told you. He has six payments left on the property. I paid off his loan and now he owes me. I'm not charging interest like the bank, so the payments are actually cheaper than he was used to. He came to me for help, and—"

"How kind of you," she stated drily.

Colt shrugged with a smile. "I thought so."

Annabelle sucked in a deep breath and dropped her hands to her sides. Stepping forward, she came within a couple feet of Colt, enough for him to see the variation of green in her eyes. Definitely eyes a man could get lost in. Not him, but some other man. Colt only did physical relationships, nothing more.

"You'll be dealing with me from now on."

Oh, he sure as hell hoped so.

"I will take over the payments, but I need you to give me a few weeks to get on my feet. I have no job, since I came back to Stone River sooner than I'd expected," she went on, a flash of sadness flickering in her eyes. "Our savings are…well, that's none of your concern. But I already called a few places this afternoon and I'm sure I'll have a job shortly."

She couldn't be playing any better into his scheme. Before he could present her with his brilliant plan, she held up her hand.

"If you can give me two weeks off initially, I'll make sure you get interest as a sign of good faith." Annabelle's lips thinned. She was furious with her old man, as she should be. "I have plans for my home, so believe me, I don't want to drag this out any longer than necessary."

Colt admired her determination. Hell, he knew all about setting sights on a goal and going straight for it. Hadn't he lived his entire life by such ideals?

The dude ranch dream he shared with his father was just the final piece of his life he needed to click into place.

There had been setbacks along the way. Colt hadn't expected his father to slip into dementia and require around-the-clock care. Colt hadn't planned on breaking his back and shattering his hip bone while rebuilding the barn after a tornado ripped through town last year. His brothers had instantly reminded him there was no need to lift a hammer, they hired their work done.

But Colt loved manual labor. He loved this farm and he wasn't about to let anyone, even his sexy neighbor, stand in the way of him taking it to the next level.

"Here's the deal." He took one step forward, closing the gap between them. Head tilted up, her eyes locked on to his. "You will make the payment on time, as was agreed by your father. One late payment and the land will permanently be mine."

It would be in the end anyway, but if a payment was missed, at least Colt would have his property sooner.

Those green eyes narrowed. "I had no idea about this deal until last night when I returned home. I've been back less than twenty-four hours. I need some time to make job arrangements before the payment is due next week. Surely you're not that coldhearted."

Part of him felt sorry for her, but he was about to extend the proverbial olive branch…whether or not she chose to accept it was on her. Either way, he would be the real winner at the end of the day.

"Not at all." He offered a smile that he knew had

brought women to their knees…literally. "I have a position for you right here at Pebblebrook."

Silence settled between them as he waited on her response. They both knew he held the upper hand, but she could make this entire encounter much easier on herself.

The muscles in her jaw clenched as she glared at him. Damn if her sass and grit weren't the sexiest things he'd seen in a long time.

Agreement or not, this woman would be in his bed. Visions of that crimson red hair spread all around his navy sheets flooded his mind. But seduction would have to wait, at least until she wasn't shooting daggers at him.

"I don't even want to know the position you think I'm qualified for."

Colt laughed, realizing he'd felt more alive being the target of her snarky attitude than he had in a long time. "I like you."

"Well, right now, I hate you."

He shrugged. "You're the yin to my yang. Sounds like we're going to get along perfectly in the stables."

"Stables?" she repeated, with a quirk of a brow.

"I'm short a stable hand and you need a job. You can start tomorrow and I'll use your wages toward the payments."

Annabelle pulled in a breath and shook her head. "I can't work long hours. I have another commitment and I need a job that offers some flexibility."

He leaned forward, pleased when her eyes flared. "The way I see it, you don't really have a choice. So, if this other obligation is going to get in the way, I suggest you give it up now."

For a split second Colt was convinced she was going to cry. He didn't like being played and he figured she'd try to get his sympathy by weeping. But when she blinked and glanced away, Colt realized she was simply trying to control herself.

Yeah, Annabelle was quite a strong woman to come here and face her father's problem. Colt despised the man for putting his child in such a position. Everyone had their breaking point and Colt figured she'd dealt with her father's addiction for far too long.

The strength she projected was quite the turn-on. Too bad all this business got in the way of him getting her into his bedroom. Soon, he vowed.

"Whatever this other commitment is, you're going to have to let it go."

She shoved her hair behind her shoulders and turned her attention back to him. "I can't. I will work here, but you have to understand there are times I will have to adjust my schedule. I can give you a few hours at a time."

Colt considered her ultimatum. He wasn't one to give in to demands, but he had to admit, he liked what he saw with his new neighbor. Someone with that much grit would be a fun way to break up his days. Besides, remaining somewhat on her good side would only aid in his seduction plan.

"Fine. I'll pick you up at seven tomorrow morning," he informed her.

Annabelle laughed. "I can drive myself."

"If you hit another section of my fence, I'll have to take the repairs out of your check and you're indebted to me already. The transportation is nonnegotiable."

When she let out an extremely unladylike growl, Colt forced himself not to crack a smile. Not even a little one. He may hang out with cowboys all day and make business deals all other waking hours, but he knew how to treat a woman. His father had instilled manners in him—somewhat—and Colt wasn't about to laugh in her face. But he couldn't resist the fence jab or the scheme to get a few minutes of alone time with her each day.

"Fine," she gritted out between her teeth. "I'll be ready."

When she turned to leave, he couldn't help but take in the fine sway of her skirt and imagine what lay beneath.

"Oh, one more thing." He waited until she stopped, throwing a glance over her shoulder. "Be sure to wear old clothes. We tend to get dirty."

Her eyes flared before narrowing. "Did I mention that I hate you right now?"

"It will pass," he informed her with a smile. "See you first thing in the morning."

Three

"You don't have to do this, honey."

Annabelle pulled in a deep breath and attempted to count backward from ten. She moved off the last step and met her father's worried gaze.

Neil Carter stood next to the front door, his hair messed from more than just sleeping. She hadn't expected her father to be waiting on her so early, but that's the type of man he was. Neil may be a professional gambler, losing pretty much all he'd worked for and all he'd provided, but he loved his family. He'd been the rock when her mother passed while Annabelle and her sister had been in grade school—well, until it all became too much and he turned to gambling. But he hurt, too, and Annabelle knew he was devastated after Trish's death only weeks ago. They both were. But for now, she could only deal with one crisis at a time.

The mourning would have to come later, at least for her…because she had to get over the betrayal first and she truly didn't even know if that was possible.

"I do have to do this, dad." Now was not the time to get into her arrangement with Colt, not when her ride was due any minute. "You left me no choice since we have no other way to pay."

Her father had lost his job at the factory one county over when he couldn't make it to work on time. He'd been embarrassed to tell her, but now that she was back, there was no way to hide anything. She needed to be aware of every ugly truth so she could make things right.

Her father raked a hand down his face and stared up at the ceiling. "I'm sorry, baby girl."

Wasn't he always sorry after the fact? This time, though, she had to put her life on hold and dig them both out of this hell. She didn't know what he would've done had she not come home.

"I can't do this right now, Dad. Between you and Colt, I'm pretty stuck. But we'll get through this."

"I'll talk to him," her father vowed, his gaze seeking her once more. "I can make this work, Belle. I can stop gambling. I'll get another job and help out. I know you and—"

"No." She held up a hand, not ready for him to take this conversation in another direction or make promises he couldn't keep. "We're going to be fine. I'll still do everything I'd planned to, it's just going to be on a different timeline."

As in, years away. The family life, the bed-and-breakfast...those plans would have to wait.

The doorbell rang and Annabelle jerked her attention to the old oak door. Her father turned, but Annabelle stepped forward to cut him off.

"I'll get it." Closing the space between them, she put her hand on her dad's shoulder. "Maybe you shouldn't be in here right now."

"But—"

"No. You and I will talk, but not now and you're not talking to Colt. You've done enough."

Her father cringed, but she refused to feel guilty. This was a mess—a mess he'd gotten them into. Perhaps he needed a dose of reality.

Finally, her father nodded and headed toward the steps. Annabelle waited until he was gone before she pulled in a breath and opened the front door.

Colt stood on her porch with his black hat in hand, as if he were there to ask her on a date. Damn that man. As if his Southern charm and manners would make her not loathe him on sight.

But he was a sight to behold. A black T-shirt stretched across his broad shoulders and those well-worn jeans fit in all the right places. She'd never seen a finer cowboy. If she were to pass Colt on the street, she'd never guess him to be a billionaire rancher who swooped in and stole properties while trying to charm the panties off unsuspecting women. There was no way he didn't have his own agenda with her family's land, and regarding this little matter of him giving her a ride. If that wasn't the worst use of a euphemism, she didn't know what was.

Colt raked his eyes over her and she forced herself not to fidget. Someone like Colt probably had eye candy for every night of the week, one on each arm. No doubt leggy blondes with big hair and big boobs, hanging on his every word. They probably wore booty shorts and cowgirl boots, too.

"I see you dressed for the day."

She'd found her oldest jeans and a simple tank. Any girl from Texas had a great pair of worn boots, so she'd thrown those on and pulled her hair into a ponytail. No makeup, no fuss. She was there to save her home, not get marks for her grooming.

Behind her, Annabelle heard the familiar sounds she'd grown to love over the past few months. Before she could turn or say a word, Colt's gaze widened and she knew exactly what he saw.

Not that she wanted him to have any part of her personal life, but she was pleased to render him speechless for a bit. Maybe Colt Elliott could be shaken and knocked down a peg.

"And who are these pretty girls?" he asked, still keeping his eyes over her shoulder.

Annabelle smiled. "Emily and Lucy. My twins."

Colt was rarely at a loss for words, but seeing Neil hold two mini versions of Annabelle was quite shocking. She hadn't mentioned having a baby—or babies. Now he understood why she needed a flexible work schedule…and he felt like a complete jerk.

Twins were definitely a handful. He should know, considering his mother always said that about him and his brother Beau. Colt wondered how Annabelle thought she could work and manage two infants back at home, but—

No. He wasn't going to get involved. Business and seduction were the only items on his agenda.

But could he still seduce her? Was she taken? There hadn't been a ring on her finger and she'd never said anything about having a husband...not that he'd asked her any such thing.

Annabelle turned, crossed the foyer and kissed each girl on the cheek. Instantly, one of the girls reached for Annabelle, but she shook her head.

"I'll be home soon. I love you both."

As she came back to him, one baby started to fuss, which somehow triggered the other one to start whimpering. Annabelle kept walking until she was out the door. With his hands full of unhappy infants, Neil held on to Colt's gaze, but Colt didn't feel a bit guilty. That man had done some major damage to his family...damage Colt hoped Annabelle never found out about. He'd lost their home and that was bad enough. But there was more and it was certainly not Colt's place to share.

He closed the door behind him, settled his hat back on his head and turned to Annabelle. She swiped at her cheeks, as if he didn't notice the tear tracks.

Guilt punched him in the chest.

"Where's the truck?" she asked, obviously not wanting to address her emotions.

Fine. He wasn't one to get in touch with his emotions, either. Just another area he realized they may be more alike than he'd care to admit. They both clearly had a love for their family and were determined to get what they wanted.

But only one of them would be the winner in the end…and he never lost.

Colt stepped off the porch, making mental notes to expand its width and put in a stone walkway when the place was officially his. He needed to stay focused on the goal. While this house had good bones and was fine for everyday living, Colt wanted it to be up to the standards of his ranch. If they were going to merge the properties and open it to the public, all homes had to be similar in upgrades.

Colt nodded toward the side of the house. "I didn't bring my car."

Walking ahead of him, Annabelle rounded the house and stopped. "You've got to be kidding me?"

Colt shook his head. "She needed a walk, so we're taking him."

Annabelle stood next to Lightning and glared his way. "I'm not riding with you."

Glancing around, he held his arms out, palms up. "I don't see another horse. Do you have one?"

Her lips thinned. He knew damn well she had no animals. Her father had sold them all.

"I seriously hate you," she murmured.

Yeah, he got that. But Colt also saw how she looked at him. She may hate his actions, but she appreciated him as a man and he was more than fine with that.

Keeping things physical would assure that everything stayed simple.

When he stepped forward to help her up, she shot him a stare that could've frozen hell over. He held up his hands to signal that he was backing off.

Hands on her hips, Annabelle stared at the horse as if weighing her options. She had none really.

"I'll just drive," she told him.

"That wasn't part of our deal. Get on the horse."

Her hand went to the reins. "Do you ever ask people nicely?"

"I can be very nice, Annabelle." He stepped closer. His hand covered hers as her eyes widened. "Get on the horse or I'll be forced to assist you like the gentleman my father raised."

She pulled her hand from beneath his and let out a mock laugh, hoisting herself up onto the horse. "I haven't met your brothers, but you are certainly no gentleman."

Colt slid his foot through the stirrup and settled in right behind Annabelle. Her backside was nestled between his thighs and he was starting to question his own motives. He'd wanted this alone time. He'd purposely made this stipulation so he could use these moments to seduce her. The concept of riding the horse developed after the deal had been made.

Colt had no idea he'd lose grip on his power. He never thought she'd be the one seducing him…and she didn't even have a clue.

The last woman he'd let have control over his emotions had left him mentally scarred and jaded. Colt pushed aside thoughts of his ex and reached around Annabelle to grab the reins. Her entire body tensed.

"Relax." He snapped the straps lightly, sending Lightning into motion. "We're just going next door."

Which would take several minutes because of the expansive fields between their properties, and he had every intention of taking the scenic route.

"Why are you heading toward the back of the property?" she asked.

Strands from her ponytail blew in the breeze, tickling the side of his neck. Images of that hair spread all over him assaulted his mind. The floral scent from her shampoo or soap assaulted his senses. She shouldn't smell like heaven, shouldn't have the ability to affect him without saying a word.

"You've only seen this land from your side," he explained. "I'm going to familiarize you with Pebblebrook."

"I thought I was just going to be in the barns cleaning horse sh—"

"Oh, you will," he laughed. She truly despised him, yet there was a fine line between lust and hate. He'd wear her down. "There will be times you'll accompany me in the fields and you need to know the area. With five thousand acres, it's easy to get turned around. But you'll be working directly with me every day."

Her shoulders slumped. The movement was slight, but being this close, he was attuned to every aspect of her.

"And what happens at the end?" Her voice was so

low, almost defeated. "You're just going to give the property back and play hero for saving the day?"

"I'm not a hero." Her body rocked back and forth against his as he murmured into her ear. There was no way he was going to answer that question outright. "I do have motives, but we don't have to talk about that right now."

Annabelle jerked around. "I knew you weren't doing any of this out of the kindness of your black heart."

Facing the open fields once again, she asked, "So why this game with my father?"

"I'm not a complete bastard, Annabelle." Though some would say otherwise. "I'm giving your father a chance to redeem himself. I don't think he can, but everyone deserves a second chance."

"You weren't expecting me to come home."

"A minor glitch, but a pleasant surprise," he replied as he neared the fence line separating the two properties.

"This isn't a game, Colt." She glanced back over her shoulder, her deep green eyes piercing his. "You're playing with our lives, my dreams."

His father had dreams as well, and Colt was going to see them through no matter what sultry beauty stood in his way. Business first, seduction second—and nothing else mattered.

"I'm fully aware of the stakes," he informed her. "I have a vision, too."

"To toy with people's lives and count your money?"

He couldn't blame her for being angry. He'd feel the same if he were in her position. But he'd never let himself get into this predicament. His land was his life. From the time he was a toddler with his first set of boots and shiny belt buckle, he knew ranching was the only future he wanted. His brothers all set out in different paths, but Colt wanted to stay right here. And yes, money was a nice byproduct of the lifestyle he loved so much.

All the Elliott boys had grown up with a rather lavish lifestyle. They were all doing what they loved, but they'd also been handed a handsome inheritance when their grandfather passed away. Still, regardless of their last name, they worked hard and played hard.

"You aren't the only one with goals," he stated as he steered Lighting toward his brother's house, settled in the back of the property. "That log home back there is Nolan's."

She may not care about his family, but she was going to be working for him and he took his ranch very seriously. At the end of the day, regardless of the fact he wanted her physically, she would have to do the job he hired her for.

When she remained silent, he kept going. "He's the oldest. He'll help occasionally, but he's a surgeon so his time is limited."

"He sounds nice."

Colt agreed, even though her comment was a jab at him. "I have another brother, Hayes. He's in the army."

"Wow. Two brothers who give back and help others, then you who steal. We haven't even discussed your movie star brother."

Colt swallowed. "My twin, Beau. He rarely comes home. Ranch life was never for him."

Beau and Colt never saw eye to eye on most things, but they had a special bond. Colt loved Beau, even though he wished he would've stuck around. Apparently fame was more important than family.

"Sounds like they made wiser life decisions."

Colt had developed thick skin over the years. He couldn't be in the ranching industry and not toughen up. But he wasn't about to sit there and have her question his integrity or his purpose.

"My grandfather built the first house on Pebblebrook, the one Hayes lives in when he's home. Then he passed this land down to my father who ended up building the house I live in. We all work hard, Annabelle. We do what we love, we make good money, and that's nothing to be sorry for."

Once again, those green eyes turned to him. "No, you have plenty of other things to be sorry for."

Perhaps he did. Maybe he was no better than her father who'd put her in this position. Colt didn't want to expose his reasons for paying the loan. The fact she knew he had a motive was enough for now. A wise businessman never showed his entire hand from the get-go.

Annabelle hated him, that was definitely no secret. But he wasn't backing down. Not on the land and certainly not on the woman.

Four

Annabelle absolutely loathed being on this horse with Colt. Well, her body enjoyed the ride, but that physical reaction didn't mean a thing. So what if his body fit perfectly against hers? So what if his voice tickled her ear and sent shivers through her? She could handle that. She had bigger issues to deal with than her body's unwanted reaction.

Colt seemed like such a normal guy in some ways. When he discussed his family there was such love, such adoration. The love and adoration she had for her own family had been shattered, broken, and she was left to pick up the shards and attempt to piece them back together.

The twins were the one bright spot in all of this chaos. They were precious, innocent, and Annabelle intended to keep them protected from the worries she faced. They would have a stable family life, maybe not the traditional family she longed for, but what was traditional these days?

Circling back to her more lustful thoughts, Annabelle couldn't ignore the tingle each time his body rocked against hers. That broad, strong chest would brush her back, his muscular forearms aligning with hers. His tanned skin to her pale. They were completely opposite in every way imaginable.

Colt Elliott was a gorgeous man, there was no denying that fact. He was also arrogant, frustrating, and the bane of her existence.

"I'm sorry to hear about your sister." Colt's words broke through her thoughts, and he actually sounded sincere. "I know you don't want to hear it from me, but losing a family member is hard."

Harder when there was betrayal involved.

She didn't want his pity or his kind words. She couldn't afford to accept that there may be a nice bone in his body. "I'm more concerned with my father and how he will handle the loss."

"That's why you came back?"

Annabelle swallowed. "One of the reasons. My fiancé and I had plans, but…"

She was so not getting into this with him. She didn't want to talk about how her entire life had blown up in her face over the past few months. The only bright spots were Emily and Lucy, and everything Annabelle did from here on out was for those sweet angels.

"I didn't realize you were engaged."

Pain pierced her heart, but not necessarily because she thought he'd been the one. Looking back now she realized she wasn't in love with him so much as the idea of being in love. She wanted to be a wife and mother, come back to Stone River and open her bed-and-breakfast.

She'd always wondered about fulfilling her mother's dream, but over the past year, she'd decided to just go for it. Yet now she was stuck in an arrangement with Colt, who, despite massive personality flaws, had more sex appeal than should be legal. Annabelle had to get her life back on track. She couldn't handle this lack of control and uncertainty.

"My fiancé is no longer in the picture."

Even with the bright morning sun beating down on them, she shivered. The pain, the loss, the trust she'd once had in people she loved was all too much. This topic wasn't bearable.

"How many acres did you say you have?"

"Just over five thousand. There are three homes, mine, Nolan's, and Hayes's, for when he's stateside. We have seven ponds and eight barns."

Pebblebrook was like a city in itself. Annabelle would be lying if she didn't admit that she was jealous. Not that she wanted a large spread like this, she'd be so content with getting her bed-and-breakfast up and running. Still, she was envious that Colt had known exactly what he'd wanted, apparently from the time he was a kid, and had accomplished it all. Granted, the majority had been handed to him, but Colt had stepped up as part of the new generation to lead the ranch to the next level and beyond.

Anger bubbled within her. He had it all and he still wanted more. She wasn't about to go down without a fight. The bed-and-breakfast, her childhood home, was all she had to make something of her life and to secure a stable future for Emily and Lucy. So whatever he had in his head about her land, he could think again.

"Do you plan on taking me back and forth several times a day?" she asked, glancing back at him.

She hated looking over her shoulder because each time she did, she saw that sexy scruff along his jaw-line and those striking blue eyes. Not to mention the movement pressed her lower half deeper into the V of his thighs. It was like this man was created to drive her out of her ever-loving mind.

And she couldn't forget the fact she'd seen him sans shirt. Like that was an image she'd ever forget. Colt Elliott had embedded himself in her deepest fantasies... not that he would ever know.

"If I'm not around, I will have Ryan or Josh take you. They are my most trusted employees."

"It's a ride home, Colt."

His bright blue eyes zeroed in on hers, then dropped to her lips for the briefest of seconds. "They're both married."

"Just because they're married doesn't mean they're committed," she countered, hating the bitterness in her tone. "And I can take care of myself. I'm working for you, I'm not a little sister you need to watch over."

A corner of his mouth kicked up in a naughty grin that had her toes curling in her boots. "Considering my thoughts, it's best we aren't related in any way."

Annabelle jerked back around, her heart beating double time in her chest. "You aren't going to flirt with me, Colt. I'm here to make sure those payments are made on time and I get to keep my house. So whatever it is you're thinking, keep it to yourself."

"But you'd enjoy every one of my thoughts," he whispered in her ear.

The brush of his lips along her cheek sent tremors racing through her. How could she hate him and be so turned on at the same time? This man stood in the way of her only chance at a stable future.

No, her father had stood in the way, Colt was just an extra hurdle she had to jump. She really didn't want to be one of those bitter, scorned women, but every man in her life had let her down. Why the hell would she expect any different from her new employer?

Besides, he was just trying to throw her off her game. And, damn it, it was working. She had to be sharper from here on out…and he needed to keep his shirt on.

"Let's just stick to business," she suggested as they neared a massive two-story barn.

She forced herself not to gape at the large stone archway that led into the tunnel where the horses were kept. The wide planked sides were weathered, but in that deliberate, expensive way. A smaller door up top no doubt led to the hayloft.

Annabelle couldn't help but wonder how many women Colt and his sexy, Southern charms had seduced up into that romantic space. She vowed not to be one of them. She wasn't naive. She knew he looked at her with interest, but she and her fiancé hadn't even consummated their relationship, and she sure as hell wasn't going to let Colt Elliott charm her into bed.

"These are the stables for our older horses. We have two mares and three stallions housed here. Ryan tends to oversee this group."

A man in a fitted plaid shirt stepped through the doorway, leading a gorgeous black stallion by the reins.

Colt steered Lightning toward the barn. As they neared, the forty-something man turned toward them.

"Ryan, this is Annabelle Carter," Colt said. "She's going to be working with me for the foreseeable future."

"Ma'am." Ryan nodded with the tip of his hat. "Pleasure to meet you. Colt, the engineer called earlier and needs you to call when you get a chance."

"I'll do it this afternoon," Colt replied.

Every time he spoke, the rumble in his chest vibrated against her back. There was something entirely too intimate about this situation. The way she fit so perfectly between his thighs, the way her body heated that had nothing to do with the sun, the way he looked at her mouth like he wanted to devour her.

And she knew without a doubt he'd methodically planned this mode of transportation and made it nonnegotiable just so he could annoy her further. Added to that, he must be well respected because his employee didn't bat an eye at the sight of the new recruit and the way she'd arrived on the scene.

"Also, Monte from the feed store called and our truckload will arrive around two this afternoon."

"We'll unload it in the barn on the west side. Make sure to tell Josh. We need all hands for that."

Ryan nodded once again and tugged on the reins of his horse. "Nice to meet you, ma'am."

He climbed onto the stallion and headed around the side of the barn.

"He seems nice. It's strange how the two of you get along."

"You're hurting my feelings, Belle."

She cringed. "Don't call me that."

"What do you prefer? Annabelle suits you, but it's a mouthful. Besides, I want my own name for you."

"Ms. Carter would work fine. Or, you don't have to refer to me at all."

That low chuckle sent even more tremors through her, causing her body to respond in ways she did not want where Colt was concerned.

"Oh, come on now, Belle. That's no way to start your first workday."

Fisting her hands on the horn of the smooth saddle, Annabelle forced herself to take calm, deep breaths. "I offered to get a different job, I'd prefer a different job, actually. I just needed some time to start getting a paycheck."

"I can give you time, but then you'd lose your land."

"Isn't that your ultimate goal anyway? To see my father and me fail? I'm not naive, Colt. I figure you want our property for something."

"I don't like to see anyone fail," he corrected as he led them toward the front of the property. "But if I'm going to be in a fight, I want it to be fair so my victory is that much sweeter."

A fight. She had to remember that's exactly what this was with him. She was fighting for her life, her future.

All she'd wanted was to take her meager savings and start minor renovations on her house to bring it up to par for her dream.

But then life had intervened. Her sister and fiancé were taken away, Annabelle found herself an instant mother to twin babies, and her father had ultimately failed her when she'd needed him most.

She wasn't going to fail him, though. He was hurting. He'd lost his daughter, was trapped in his own hell with his addiction, and Annabelle would fight to the death if necessary to keep her family safe. She would make a home for Emily and Lucy, take back her land, and see the B and B come to fruition. Anything less was not an option.

Colt Elliott may have knocked her down a peg, but she was determined to fling him off his podium.

Colt's shoulders burned, his arms strained as he hoisted the last bag of feed onto the pile he and Ryan had created. Josh had been taking loads and dispersing them to other barns.

And Annabelle had been holding her own. Sweat had her little tank clinging to her back. Damp tendrils of hair had escaped her ponytail and were now plastered against her neck. She'd gone home for lunch and had returned just before the shipment had arrived. He'd been busy and asked Ryan to take her and bring her back...using the truck.

But there was no way he was missing an opportunity to deliver her back home. They'd worked hard and he was utterly exhausted. He could only imagine how she felt as someone who wasn't used to this type of work every day.

He had a walk-in shower with three rain heads and jetted sprays waiting on him. Not to mention a bottle of bourbon he'd just acquired from a special selection that had been aging in a barrel for decades. He loved his contacts in Kentucky.

Guilt nipped at his conscience. When Annabelle went home, she had two babies to take care of and he highly doubted she took any downtime for herself.

Annabelle continued stacking boxes from the pallets into the corner of the barn. She didn't once stop to look his way, didn't say a word, and didn't complain. She was already a better employee than the stable hand he'd fired last week…only she wasn't a regular employee. She was there under duress, against everything she wanted.

Part of him wanted to tell her to go, to let her father handle the mess he'd made, but he knew she wouldn't go for that. She was too proud, too loyal to her family. She'd lost her sister and her father had completely let her down. And from her tone when she'd briefly mentioned her fiancé, he'd let her down, too. Colt had to assume the man was the twins' father, but he honestly had no clue…and it wasn't his right to ask.

The more tidbits into her life he discovered and pieced together, the more admiration he had for her.

"That's the last of it," Ryan stated.

Colt pulled his hat off, swiped his forehead with his

arm and turned to Ryan. "Go ahead and take off. I'll finish up here."

"Want me to give her a lift on my way out?" Ryan asked, nodding toward Annabelle on the other end of the barn.

"I'll take care of her, as well."

Ryan eyed Colt and he knew what was coming.

"Don't say it."

Ryan merely shrugged. "Someone needs to. You're playing with fire."

Oh, he sure as hell hoped so. Was there any other way to play a game of seduction?

"I know what I'm doing."

Ryan's brows lifted. "Do you? Because your father may have had a vision, but he wouldn't have put someone through this just to gain the land."

Colt jerked his work gloves off and shoved them into his back pocket. "Which is why she'll be with me. I won't let her do more than she's capable of."

"Did you know her hand was bleeding?" Ryan asked.

Colt jerked his attention toward her once again. "What?"

"When I walked by earlier, she was wiping her hand on her pants and I saw blood. She'd torn her work gloves."

Damn stubborn woman wouldn't ask for help no matter what.

"I got her another pair," Ryan went on. "But I have a gut feeling she'd fall over before she came to one of us for help."

That she would. Colt raked a hand over the back of

his neck and nodded. "I'll make sure that doesn't happen again."

"That land is going to be yours regardless," Ryan added in a low whisper. "Why don't you just let her go?"

Reasons he couldn't even explain. When she'd shown up yesterday morning and literally busted through his ranch, he hadn't been able to take his eyes off her. He'd always gone after what he wanted—livestock, business deals, employees…women.

Annabelle Carter was a total game changer.

Colt kept his eyes on Annabelle as she stacked her last box. Guilt slammed into him when she pulled off her glove and examined her hand.

Without glancing at Ryan, Colt said, "See you in the morning."

His trusted worker wisely walked away. Colt moved across the cobblestone walkway, closing the distance between him and Annabelle.

"Why didn't you tell me you were hurt?"

She spun around, clearly startled. "I'm fine."

With a hand to her chest, she tipped that defiant chin. Damn if he didn't want to kiss her. That fire in her eyes dared him to come closer, so Colt took a step forward until they were toe to toe. He'd never backed down from a challenge and Annabelle was one fight he was enjoying…except for her injury.

Colt gently curled his fingers around her wrist and pulled her hand out so he could examine it. She had a nasty blister that had been worked too hard.

"I have a first aid kit in the office."

When he met her eyes, he was surprised anger didn't

look back at him. If anything, he saw desire. Interesting...
and useful. Passion left people weak and he'd definitely
home in on that.

Annabelle blinked, as if she realized she'd been
caught staring at him. Pulling her hand back, she held
it against her chest once again.

"I'll take care of it when I get home. I need to start
dinner."

"The hell you say?" He hadn't meant to shout, but
was she kidding? "You've worked all day."

Annabelle let out a humorless laugh. "Well, Colt, in
the real world people work, make their own meals and
tend to their families. We all can't live the life of luxury
and sit back, living the dream."

Is that how she saw him? He'd worked his ass off
taking over this ranch when his father had fallen ill.
He'd poured more blood, sweat and tears into this land
than any male in the Elliott family. Being the youngest, he always felt the need to prove himself, especially
against his brothers. How the hell could he compete
with a surgeon, a war hero and a Hollywood star? He
was a damn rancher. A billionaire, but still a man who
wore dusty boots, a worn hat that had been his father's,
and holey jeans.

"You can take two minutes and let me clean that
wound up."

When she stifled a yawn with her good hand, he
muttered a curse and stomped off to get the first aid
kit. Why did she have to be so stubborn and why did
he have to find her even more attractive because of it?

By the time he came back, she'd taken a seat on one

of the heavy wooden benches between the stone stalls. Her lids were lower and she seemed to have finally run out of steam. Perfect. Then she wouldn't be able to argue with him.

"You work harder than nearly any man I know," he told her, opening the kit.

"Does that mean I get a raise?" she asked, leaning her head against the wall behind her.

Colt laughed as he placed her hand in his palm. He swiped around the perimeter of the cut with an alcohol pad, careful not to get near the wound. He blew on her hand to dry the moisture. When she trembled, he glanced up to find her eyes on his. That shade of green never failed to kick him in the gut. She could pierce a man with that stare and have him wound in her web so fast, he'd have no idea he was caught until it was too late.

"I know you hate me, but you really shouldn't be fighting your father's battles."

A sad smile crossed her face. "Isn't that what family is all about? When one is weak, others stand up and take the lead. We're all we have left. My mother passed when Trish and I were younger. Now that Trish is gone…"

She shook her head and he wanted to know so much more. When he'd wanted a woman in the past, he'd never asked personal information. Backstory had no place in the bedroom. He had to remember that here because he could so easily let this niggle of guilt guide his emotions.

He had a goal. He had a vision he would see to the end, to honor his father, to prove to his brothers he wasn't just playing cowboy and to prove to himself he could do it. The dude ranch was only one more business deal away…he just had to get past this fiery vixen to make that vision a reality.

Five

"What the hell, Colt?"

Nolan slammed the office door, jerking Colt's attention from his empty tumbler. He was going to need another round because he'd been waiting on his oldest brother to show up and let him know exactly what his thoughts were on Annabelle.

Gripping the glass, Colt met his brother's angry gaze. "All right, get it out of your system."

"Did you think to ask my opinion—"

"Not once."

Nolan crossed the room and flattened his palms on the glossy desk. "You have Neil Carter's daughter working here for what purpose?"

"He owes me money. She confronted me and said she was taking over the payments."

"So you put her to work like some pack mule?" Nolan shouted. "Do you think Dad would want this?"

Slowly, Colt came to his feet. He refused to sit there and let his brother talk down to him. "Dad left the control of this ranch to me because I understand his vision and I'm the one who's busted my ass my entire life to stay true to it."

"Don't throw that in my face," Nolan countered.

Colt shrugged. "Simply stating a fact. I don't tell you how to do surgeries."

The muscles in Nolan's jaw ticked. Colt wasn't trying to be a jerk, but he wasn't going to be reprimanded or have his decisions second-guessed. He'd done enough doubting of his own actions...something he never did with business.

"You want this dude ranch so damn bad, but you're going about this the wrong way."

Colt grabbed his glass and headed to the bar in the corner. His hip irritated him a bit more today, but that was expected on days he worked harder. It was just one more area where he refused to give in and let life get him down.

"We need that property and Neil was about to lose it to the bank. If I hadn't stepped in, someone else would've. Besides, it's all over now and perfectly legal."

Nolan turned, crossed his arms over his chest and nodded. "I agree that someone else would've gone after that land. It's your actions afterward that I don't understand."

Colt had gone over this in his own head, as well. "At first I wanted Neil to learn a lesson and actually work

for something. Then when Annabelle showed up, hell…
I couldn't resist."

He didn't look up at his brother, didn't want to see
disappointment staring back. Colt had his reasons for
his actions and he wasn't going to be deterred by anyone…not even his oldest brother.

"I don't want to see you hurt again," Nolan stated as
he crossed the room to stand before the bar. He rested
his palms on the etched edge. "Dad would be proud of
how smooth this place is running and the growth since
he's been in the assisted living facility. You don't have
to prove anything at this point."

Colt grunted as he poured two fingers of amber liq-
uid. "I started this for him, but now it's also for me. I
want that dude ranch. I want people from all over the
world to know Pebblebrook is the greatest ranch, the
best getaway money can buy. I want to share all of this
work our family has done and if I happen to have a little
fun along the way, then so be it."

Colt held out a glass and Nolan shook his head. "I'm
on call." He took a seat on the bar stool, lacing his hands
together. "This is the first girl you've mentioned at all
since Layla."

Colt took a hearty sip. "I'm not looking to settle
down. And Layla has nothing to do with now. There's
only one thing I'm focused on and that's making the
dude ranch happen. Annabelle is working here to pay
off the debt. If she misses one payment or can't come
up with the entire sum at the end of the time frame, then
it's completely mine. But it's mine in the end anyway.

They just have to pay off their original debt. Neil paid no attention to the paperwork he signed."

Nolan stared for a minute before shaking his head. "You can handle this how you want, but I'm telling you it's a moral mistake."

With a shrug, Colt finished his glass and recapped the bottle. "I've made mistakes before. And, if Annabelle is a mistake, then she'll be the sexiest one I've ever made."

Layla had been his one and only serious relationship. He should've known it was too good to be true when she'd wanted to marry so soon after they'd started dating. Colt had thought she was interested in him and shared a passion for the farm. She'd shared a passion all right...for his bank account. She didn't care about the land, the animals, his vision. She cared about how she could keep up with the latest trends in clothes, vacations, cars. Colt had been completely blind and eager to give her anything she wanted.

When he'd had an accident and been laid up with broken bones post-surgery, he found out all too quickly just how little she cared about him. She'd told him she needed a break from their lifestyle and then jetted off to his vacation home in Aruba...with another guy. If Colt's cleaning service hadn't told him, the joke would still be on him.

While recovering from surgery, Colt broke off the relationship, kicked Layla and her stud out of his house and sold the place, deciding he didn't like the beach anyway. He needed nothing but his home in Texas. He loved to travel, but what did he need a second home for? His jet and his pilot would take him anywhere he wanted to go.

He was finished with romantic entanglements and refused to get sidetracked by such emotions as love. Hell, he hadn't even been in love with Layla. He'd wanted a family one day and he figured he and Layla were the best match. He still carried that goal of having a wife and children. There was nothing he wanted more than to raise another generation of Elliotts and keep the ranching tradition going. Family and loyalty were everything to him.

He'd let his libido guide him once before, but now he knew exactly what he was feeling. Everything inside him that flared to life around Annabelle was pure lust. He wanted her, he'd have her. End of story.

"Is this necessary?" Annabelle asked.

Colt held tight to the reins, his body aligning perfectly with hers. She hadn't just dreamed of his strength. When she'd woken in the middle of the night after a vivid, detailed dream regarding her new employer, she'd thought her imagination had just gotten the best of her.

But now she knew better. She'd tried to avoid his touch yesterday, but being on horseback with him made that impossible. Maybe it was time Annabelle renegotiated this whole pickup routine.

"It's a perfect day for a ride," he replied.

His low, soft tone was in direct contrast to the chaos she felt inside. She wanted to continue hating him, and she would, but why did she have to be attracted to him at the same time? It truly made for some mixed up hormones and she couldn't keep eating her weight in doughnuts like she wanted to. Her favorite jeans were already snug as it was.

"I'd be fine to drive myself," she retorted, keeping her eyes on the bright horizon, as opposed to focusing on the proximity of his hands to her inner thighs. "Or Josh or Ryan can take over delivery duties."

"I'm a hands-on employer," he murmured against her ear. "You'll get used to it."

That was the problem. This was day two in her duties and she could honestly say she didn't hate this part. She wanted to hate it. She wanted to stomp her foot like a toddler and declare her independence by not getting on that horse with him.

But she was still a woman. Despite her jaded view on men and their loyalties, and ignoring the fact Colt had her in a tough position, she was a woman with basic desires. And her body felt exactly the way it should when a sexy man entered the scene: tingly, hot, achy.

"You're thinking awfully hard about something," he stated. "You tensed up on me."

"Just counting down the days until we're free of each other and I can go about my life with my house."

"You've still got quite a while. I wouldn't be making those plans just yet."

Annabelle shrugged. "I'm optimistic. I know I won't miss a payment and I have every reason to keep going, even if I want to give up."

She felt her hair shift aside seconds before his fingertips trailed across the back of her neck. Annabelle jerked to glance over her shoulder.

"What are you doing?"

His mouth was only inches from hers and completely tempting, so she focused back on the fence line dividing the properties. It had to be a sign, a symbol of exactly how different they were and how she needed to compartmentalize their arrangement.

"Your hair tickled my face. Why didn't you put it in a ponytail?"

She held up her wrist. "I have my band here. I didn't get time before you arrived because Emily was sick last night and I was trying to get her sheets washed and put back on the crib so Dad could lay her down for a nap later."

Why had she told him all of that? He had no place in her personal life.

"You could've texted me to give you an extra five minutes."

"That would've made me late. You're not going to win that easily, Colt. Just forget I said anything," she quickly added. "I'm not looking for sympathy or special treatment. After this debt is paid, I'm going to pursue my dream."

"Care to share what that dream is?"

Annabelle bit the inside of her cheek and thought for a half second, but shook her head. "Nope. You've stolen enough from me. I won't give you my hopes, too."

"It's not your secrets I'm after, Anna."

Every part of her stilled. He wanted her, that was obvious. He wasn't even trying to pretend otherwise. But she wasn't about to comment on that.

"Don't call me Anna."

His soft chuckle had his entire body vibrating against hers. "I'm willing to call you anything, but you don't like any name I've chosen."

"Like I said before, maybe it would be best if you didn't address me at all, except for work purposes, and then you can call me Ms. Carter."

Colt pulled back on the reins, bringing Lightning to a stop at the edge of the property line. "And what about now, when we're alone and not working. What should I call you?"

Slowly, Annabelle turned her head slightly, knowing full well he'd eased forward and his face would be right there. And it was. Those lips mocked her, the edge of his hat bumped the top of her head, bright eyes stared back, daring her to answer the question.

"Maybe we shouldn't talk."

The instant his eyes flared, darting to her lips, she realized he took her comment as a challenge. He eased forward, his eyes locked on hers the entire time. Her mind told her to stop, but his eyes mocked her as if he knew she would. So she didn't.

His lips grazed hers and everything in her stilled. The slow caress of that mouth had her closing her eyes and forgetting who they were. For once, she was going to just take this moment of pleasure and ignore all the warning bells inside her head.

Colt eased her mouth open beneath his and Annabelle responded as if it were the most natural thing in the world. She wanted Colt's mouth on hers, she wanted him to…

No. This wasn't right. Annabelle pulled away, instantly feeling a chill from the loss of his touch.

"You can't possibly believe you're going to get anywhere with me," she stated, needing to get control back in her grasp. That kiss had only temporarily caught her off guard. Still, his body rubbed against hers, making her want things she'd never had.

"I tend to get what I want," he whispered. "And from the way you responded, I'd say we want the same thing."

She was out of her league with this one. He was charming, smart and devious. But she was determined not to succumb to his attempt at seduction. And that was exactly what he was doing, no doubt so she would lose focus and hand over her property. Not in this lifetime.

"Then I'd look elsewhere because this will never be yours."

"And you?" he asked, quirking a brow and smiling.

Anna reached around and palmed the side of his face. His jaw muscle ticked beneath her hand as she looked into his eyes.

"You won't get that lucky," she said sweetly, then patted his face before letting go. "Now get me to work."

When he didn't reach for the reins again, she lifted them, lightly tapping Lightning into motion again. Which she instantly discovered to be a mistake.

Colt's hands flattened against the tops of her denim-clad thighs. She refused to tense, refused to even comment on his actions. They'd already crossed a professional boundary, but it wasn't like this was a typical boss-employee relationship. Nothing here was normal. She had no idea how to react, what to say. All she knew was that Colt challenged her minute by minute and she had to stay on her toes and never let her guard down again.

She could still taste him, though, knew exactly how he felt, how gentle he'd been. She'd expected someone like Colt to go in full attack mode when trying to seduce a woman. It was like he knew her situation and catered specifically to her needs...her desires.

Surprisingly, he let her guide them straight to the barn. Annabelle figured his cockiness, as shown by him keeping his hands on her, overrode the need to be in control for now. But she wasn't under the illusion that he was relinquishing his power.

"What's on the agenda today?" she asked as she stopped in front of the barn.

Barn was such a generic, ridiculous term for such a structure. The interior of the barn alone rendered her speechless, she couldn't imagine what the other barns and homes on the property looked like inside.

He slid his hands over hers on the reins. "You and I will be going out and checking the fence lines around the property. I tend to have Josh and Ryan do that, but I'm giving your hands a break after yesterday."

The warmth from his touch, the way he literally enveloped her would be so easy to get caught up in if this were any other type of situation. But he was the main obstacle standing between her and her bed-and-breakfast, and the life she wanted for Emily and Lucy.

Annabelle worried Colt had something up his sleeve...something she wouldn't see coming until it was too late.

"I don't want special treatment. My hand is just fine." Sore, but she'd put some antibiotic ointment and a bandage on it. "Treat me like you would any other stable hand."

Colt grunted. "That's not going to happen."

He eased off the horse, then extended a hand to assist her. "I can get down myself."

As she slid off the side, firm hands gripped her waist. "A gentleman always helps a lady."

Annabelle turned in his arms and placed her hands on his chest. A very firm, solid, muscular chest. She pulled in a deep breath and forced herself to focus.

"If you're trying to seduce me, it won't work." But it could if she didn't keep giving herself mental pep talks. He had to keep those lips to himself, though. "And if you're trying to make this process more difficult, then don't waste your time. I'm not backing down and I'm not quitting. So, tell me where I'm working today and knock off the shenanigans."

He pursed his lips and she knew from that naughty twinkle in his bright eyes that he was holding back a laugh. With a tip of his hat, he took a step back.

"Then that goes both ways."

Shocked, Annabelle held a hand to her chest. "Excuse me?"

"No seducing me. I know, it will be tough to control yourself around me, but try. I'm not just here for my looks."

When he let go and offered a full smile, she smacked his shoulder. "Get out of my way, you arrogant jerk. I will not seduce you. I'm sure a number of women find you charming, but I am certainly not one of them."

Annabelle started to move, but he snaked an arm around her waist. Bringing his lips next to her cheek, he whispered, "You will be."

Before she could reply, he turned and headed into the barn. As if she weren't irritated enough, the man had the gall to start whistling. Annabelle gritted her teeth and fisted her hands at her sides.

Colt Elliott was not going to get under her skin. She would not find that arrogance attractive, nor would she allow herself to feel any more attraction to the sexy cowboy. She'd been burned too many times and if she didn't keep her guard up, she'd find herself hurt more than ever before.

Maybe it was time to give Colt a little dose of his own medicine.

Six

"I think Genesis will be the perfect mare for you to use while you're here."

Annabelle slid her hand down her new friend's velvety nose. Josh had pulled this mare from her stall when Annabelle came in to find Colt and give him a piece of her mind. But he was nowhere to be found. Probably off in some corner plotting on new ways to drive her out of her mind—and off her land—with that killer body of his. If he strutted in there with no shirt, she wasn't so sure she'd be able to resist.

Mercy, when had she gotten so pathetic and weak? An impressive collection of muscles only went so far... and she had too much in her life to get distracted.

"She's beautiful." Annabelle looked into the mare's deep brown eyes. "I miss riding."

When she'd been younger, she and her sister both had
horses. Their father would take them riding nearly every
day, especially during the time when their mother was
ill. But then her mom had passed and soon her dad's
gambling began, the debts piled up and the horses were
sold. Their lives had crumbled so quickly, there wasn't
even time to adjust.

She wanted to hate her father, she truly did. She
hated the decisions he'd made, she hated his addiction,
but she loved him and she wasn't about to give up.

"I believe you and Colt will be riding the perimeter
today," Josh went on. "Looks like your face got a little
pink from working outside yesterday."

Instinctively, Annabelle tapped a fingertip to her
cheek. "Yeah, a little. I thought I had used enough sun-
screen."

"I can get you a hat," Josh told her as he looped the
reins around the horn. "We have plenty in the office."

"I've got one right here."

Annabelle turned at the sound of Colt's voice. He
came sauntering up the stone walkway, hat in hand.
That flutter in her chest had her cursing. How could she
be strong when he made her want so much? She'd never
been this drawn to a man physically. Even her fiancé
hadn't given her that nervous flutter in her stomach.

Why did it have to be the one man she wanted to
hate? And why did he have to do little things to make
it seem as if he actually had redeeming qualities?

"Ryan is in the steer barn," Colt said to Josh. "There's
a calf that isn't looking good. I called the vet, but I'd

like if both of you were there. Take the radio with you and keep me informed."

"Sure thing." Josh glanced at Annabelle and nodded. "See you later."

She waited until they were alone before she turned her attention back to Colt. "Do you ever ask anyone politely or do you just enjoy ordering people around?"

"I have a busy schedule and those guys don't need coddling." Colt slapped the hat on her head. "If you have a problem with how I run my ranch, you're free to go at any time."

Annabelle adjusted the hat, narrowing her eyes. "You know I can't."

"Then stop trying to school me on manners. My guys and I get along just fine and run this place quite successfully."

Annabelle's phone vibrated inside her pocket. She pulled it out, glanced at the screen, then looked at Colt. "I have to take this."

She didn't wait for his reply as she swiped her finger over the screen. "Dad, this isn't a great time. Can I call you back in a bit?"

"I think Emily has a fever."

Annabelle pinched the bridge of her nose and willed herself to remain calm. She had no experience with sick babies. She was still getting used to being a guardian, but she would always put them first. Before the farm and before her father's addiction. She adored those babies, hated when she was away from them. They were a balm on her battered heart.

Annabelle could tell by the concern in her father's

tone that she had to keep a level head, even if worry flooded her. Between the two of them, they were still figuring out their new normal.

"When I fed her around four this morning she was fine. Did you take her temperature?"

Boots shifted over stone behind her and Annabelle tried to block out the fact that Colt was no doubt clinging to her every word. Again, she didn't want him involved in her personal business any further.

Cooing in the background brought her back to reality. If Emily was getting sick, Annabelle didn't want the girls close together. The last thing anyone needed was two sick infants.

"I can't find a thermometer."

"Go into my room and look in the top nightstand drawer. I have one in there as well as some infant pain reliever. Take her temperature and call me right back."

She disconnected the call and turned back around. Colt's eyes studied her, as if he were waiting on her to open up about the call and her life. Not likely.

Colt took a step forward. "Do you need to go back home?"

"I'm fine." A little worried, but she'd never let him see it and this was none of his concern.

"Take Genesis and go check on Emily."

Before she could answer, her phone vibrated in her hand. "Dad," she quickly answered. "What was it?"

"It's 99.9."

Okay, not terrible. "Give her a dose of that medicine. Just measure it in the dropper. The dosage is on the back for her weight. Is she acting okay? How's Lucy?"

"Lucy is perfectly fine. Emily seems more tired than usual, but she's not cranky."

"That's good," Annabelle muttered. "Just keep me posted. Even if it's to say she's still fine, I want you to text me updates until I get back for lunch."

"All right. And, Belle," he added softly. "I'm sorry. For all of this."

Tears pricked her eyes. He was always sorry, and she truly believed for the moment that he was. Only time would tell if losing everything could really change a man. So far, since she'd been home, she hadn't seen any signs of his habits returning, but that didn't mean anything. He'd always managed to sneak some game, race or sporting event. He'd gamble on the color of the sky if that was an option. Neil Carter never turned down a bet.

"I'll be home in a few hours."

As she slid her phone in her pocket, Colt continued to study her. "Nolan is home this morning. Do you want me to send him over?"

"The doctor?" Annabelle asked. Part of her was touched that he offered, but she didn't want anything from Colt or his family…other than her house back. But, if Emily got worse, she wouldn't turn down at-home care…especially since she couldn't afford a doctor. "Emily will be fine."

Colt stared another minute before reaching up onto Genesis and pulling the reins down. "Then you have work to do."

Annabelle led the mare from the barn before mounting her. Why was Colt being so nice? The hat so her face wouldn't burn, the simple day so her hand wouldn't hurt,

the offer to send his brother over to check on Emily...
all of that showed there was a kindhearted man inside.
But he still made no apologies for planning to take over
her land or trying to seduce her.

When Colt came up beside her, she kept her eyes
on the horizon. He'd opted to take Phantom out today
instead of Lightning. All of his horses were gorgeous
animals. Annabelle couldn't pick a favorite. They were
all so well mannered, so loving.

Pebblebrook was a beautiful spread, there was no denying that. Colt was obviously passionate about ranching. She was curious about his limp, there had to be a
story there, but he'd never mentioned it or acted like it
hindered his work. And she couldn't help but wonder
why he was still single. Not that she cared, but he was
rather blatant with his advances toward her. Which reminded her, she could play that game, too.

"Lead the way, Boss."

He threw her a glance before getting Phantom into
gear. Annabelle followed to the side, staying back just
enough to appreciate the view—the land and the cowboy.

As he headed toward the fence that ran as far as the
eye could see, Annabelle started thinking, remember-
ing. There was a time she'd wondered what the other
side of this fence held. She'd wondered about the family who lived here, the house they must love and the
number of people who must work here to keep such a
place running.

Her family's farm had been minute compared to this

one, but she'd loved her animals, her childhood. She couldn't complain about the first ten years of her life.

"You're quiet back there, Belle." Colt cast a glance her way. "Plotting revenge?"

She tapped her heel into Genesis's side to come up even with Colt. "Don't call me that."

"Still waiting on you to give me something you'll answer to that doesn't sound like you're my grade school teacher."

"You'll be waiting awhile," she replied. "And I wasn't plotting revenge, not yet, anyway. I was just thinking about my own farm from when I was little."

"I didn't know you or your sister," Colt stated as he kept Phantom at a steady pace. "Our fathers knew each other, though."

"Really?" Annabelle asked. She shifted her hat to block the morning sun. "I wasn't aware of that. I don't recall Dad ever mentioning yours."

"No. He probably wouldn't have."

Confused, Annabelle slowed her horse, reached out to touch Colt's arm. "What's that supposed to mean?"

He brought Phantom to a stop and shook his head. "Exactly what I said. You were young, so I doubt your father would mention mine. That's all."

Annabelle had a gut feeling he was hiding something. Dread spread through her. Surely their fathers hadn't gambled together. People as successful as the Elliotts didn't get a ranch like this from betting their earnings away. Did her dad owe them, too?

She had to know. "Does my dad owe you all money?

Aside from the house?" She glanced down to her tight grip on the reins.

Silence settled between them and Annabelle glanced at Colt from beneath the brim of her hat. He stared out into the pasture, his jaw muscles clenching.

"How much?" she whispered.

"There's no debt other than the house."

But he wouldn't look her in the eyes, so there was something. An old debt, at least a story, and he didn't want to tell her. Was he protecting her?

Damn it. She'd only been with him two days and already he showed her more good sides than bad. But the bad outweighed the good. Didn't it?

"I want to pay you for everything he owes," she went on, needing him to understand. "I'm sure you're not the only person he's indebted to—"

"There's nothing. Let it go."

His stern tone, so final and angry, had her stopping short. Something had happened, but if she wanted to know, she'd have to go to her father and confront him. She almost didn't want to find out the truth.

They rode for another hour, randomly stopping to check the fence. Colt would type notes into his phone and Annabelle tried not to think about how he seemed like such a genuine guy. He worked hard, he obviously didn't want to upset her earlier about her father, but he wasn't sincere. He was a business shark.

As if she could forget.

They approached one of the ponds and Annabelle spotted movement amidst the cattails. She steered Genesis away from Colt and made her way over. She squinted, trying to home in on where she saw something.

"What's up?" Colt trotted beside her. "Wait, I see it."

Annabelle pulled back on her reins, but before she could hop down, Colt was off his horse and carefully moving toward the edge of the pond. He limped slightly, favoring his left side, but she wasn't about to question him.

Colt squatted down, extending his hand and muttering something Annabelle couldn't decipher. She waited, then sucked in a breath when he came to his feet. The sight of Colt cradling the cutest, chocolate-colored puppy had Annabelle climbing off her horse.

"Is this your puppy?" she asked as she approached.

He stroked the top of the puppy's head. "I've never seen this little guy before. But it's not unusual for us to have strays on the farm. People drop them off at the end of our drive all the time. Pisses me off."

"Do you think there are others?" she asked.

Colt shook his head, still staring down to the pup. "I have no idea. I would assume they'd all be together, but we'll ride around this area and see. They could be anywhere. Damn it. I hate when people treat animals like this."

Oh, no. He could not be an animal lover, too. Her emotions were still raw, still so exposed that she couldn't afford to let any more of his kindness seep in.

"Will you keep him?"

Colt met her gaze. "Do you want him?"

She hadn't thought about having a dog, but she'd always had one growing up. Honestly, over the past several years, she'd missed animals. When she'd lived in an apartment in the city, she hadn't been able to have them. She'd worked in a bakery and was gone all hours.

As she stared at the poor pup shaking, her heart went out to him. She totally could relate to being scared of what would happen next.

"I'll take him if you don't want him."

Colt nodded. "Fair enough. If you think you can handle a puppy and babies. Otherwise, I'll keep him."

Annabelle had a feeling the puppy would be the easiest aspect of her life. And having an animal that could grow up with Emily and Lucy would be precious. Plus, it was another way for Annabelle to establish roots in her home—well, it would be her home once it was paid off.

She eyed him, purposely zeroing in on his mouth. "I can handle anything."

When his nostrils flared, Annabelle reached forward in an attempt to get the pup, but Colt twisted his body away. His gaze remained on hers as he cocked his head to the side to avoid bumping their hats.

"You know exactly what happens when you play with fire," he growled.

A tingling swept through her, but she shrugged. "I've been burned before, Colt. I'm immune."

He stepped closer, easing the puppy into her arms and deliberately brushing his forearms along her chest. "You've never dealt with someone like me. You may like it."

Oh, she had no doubt. If that kiss yesterday was any indicator, she knew full well just how much she'd like it. But then she'd have to live with the consequences and she wasn't ready for anything like that. She was a forever kind of girl. If he only knew what she'd gone through with her ex and just how inexperienced she truly was...

"I'm sure I'd disappoint," she stated simply. Not because she doubted herself, but she knew, given their age difference, that he was much more experienced. There was no way she'd be able to live up to his expectations...and someone as sexy and wealthy as Colt definitely would have high expectations for a woman.

The puppy snuggled against her chest and Colt ran a bare fingertip up her arm, smiling when she shivered.

"I'm sure we'd both be thoroughly satisfied."

Why did that sound like a promise and not just a hypothetical situation?

The radio in Colt's saddlebag screeched, breaking the tension. He stared another moment before turning to grab the handset.

Annabelle cradled the dog in one arm and hoisted herself up onto her horse with the other. She listened as Josh assured Colt that the calf was going to be just fine and the vet had done a thorough workup and left antibiotics.

When Annabelle grabbed the reins and started to turn her horse, Colt jerked his gaze to hers.

"I'll be back after lunch," she told him as she trotted away.

Okay, so she was running, just via horseback. But she couldn't get into any more sexually charged talks with that man. Besides the fact that she was probably the only twenty-four-year-old virgin in the world, she would not get swept into Colt Elliott's web of charm, deceit and sex appeal. He was probably just trying to keep her sidetracked and it could very well work. But she had a larger goal in mind than just cashing in her virginity for a night with a sexy cowboy.

She'd dated guys before her fiancé, but never felt a passionate desire to get intimate. Then when Matt came along and they'd gotten engaged, she'd wanted to wait until they were married. He'd been fine with that, telling her he wanted it to be special. That bald-faced lie had made her feel special. If only she'd known he'd found her sister the better option. So here was Annabelle, nearly a quarter of a century old and untouched. That was definitely not something to brag about, so she tended to keep that tidbit of information to herself.

But for a minute, okay maybe more, she wondered what it would be like to be taken by someone so experienced, so powerful.

Annabelle held the pup a little tighter as she rode home on Genesis. She hadn't asked to take the horse, but she couldn't stand the tension simmering between her and Colt another minute.

When he'd touched her just a moment ago, her entire body had felt the zing…the same type she'd felt when he'd kissed her. What would happen if she gave in to those blatant advances and let him have his way?

If her entire future weren't hanging in the balance, she'd very likely find out.

Seven

"Your basket is ready."

Colt had just stepped into the kitchen to find Winnie, his cook and all-round awesome woman, patting the top of a picnic basket. He'd requested something extra for today and, as always, she'd delivered.

He circled the large granite island and kissed her on the cheek. "You're amazing, Winnie. I'm going to marry you one day."

She swatted him with her towel and laughed. "Get out of my kitchen, boy. It wasn't that long ago I spanked your bottom for stealing cookies before dinner."

Colt shot her a grin as he picked up the basket. "I still swipe your homemade cookies before dinner. I hope you put some in this basket."

"Of course I did."

She grunted as if he'd offended her. But Winnie Miller had been with this family for nearly forty years. Taking care of cowboys broke anyone of having thin skin.

"Mind telling me where you're taking that?" She raised a brow. "Maybe to see some lady friend?"

"Nothing so exciting," he replied as he headed toward the back patio doors.

"You're going to have to settle down and bring some babies in this house eventually," she called to his back. "Too many empty bedrooms."

Considering she had her own suite on the first floor, she knew exactly how many rooms sat empty now. With his father in the nursing home, the absolute best they could find, and his brothers gone, Colt was also aware of how lonely this house was. Winnie only stayed over on occasion, but she mostly went back to her cottage on the edge of town.

Deciding not to take Winnie's bait, Colt headed out the back doors and gripped the basket as he made his way across the concrete drive and stone path leading to the barn. Annabelle should be finishing up brushing the horses and then she'd be heading home for the day. He hadn't pressed her further when she came back after lunch. He knew he'd shaken her up with the sexual innuendos.

Part of him wanted to get a rise out of her, but there was something so sweet about her flirting, he was starting to wonder if he was out of his depth. Maybe she hadn't come up against real men before…men who wanted more from her than a nice, calm romp.

He could do slow. Clearly, by the pace he was setting to get Annabelle's property, he was a patient man when he wanted something.

He stopped short at the entrance to the barn. The sun was starting to set, casting an orange glow through the wide opening on the opposite end of the structure. Annabelle had lost her hat some time back, and her ponytail swayed against her back as she shifted with each brushstroke. Damp tendrils clung to her face. She never failed to shock him with her hard work. She didn't complain, never had a negative word—other than those directed straight at him and his character—and she seemed to care for these animals like they were her own.

But when she'd asked about her father owing money, Colt had clammed up. The way dread had laced her tone, her facial features, he just hadn't had the heart to come clean.

If it were up to him, she'd never have to know. She was already hurting enough and he was going to take her land. He couldn't deliberately add to her heartbreak.

Colt took a step into the barn, and his boots scuffing against the stone pulled Annabelle's attention toward him. Brush in hand, she gestured toward the basket he carried.

"Bringing a picnic for the horses?" she asked, going back to finish stroking the mare.

"Actually, this is for you."

Annabelle froze, throwing him a side glance. "Nice try, Romeo. I'm not having a picnic with you."

He couldn't help but smile at her immediate rejection. Good to know. Not that he wanted to have dinner with her, he was thinking more along the lines of sheets, showers, and haylofts. Besides, sharing a meal was too intimate.

"I had Winnie make dinner for you and your dad."

He set the basket down on one of the benches between the stalls. Shoving his hands in his pockets, he narrowed the space between them.

"Winnie?" Annabelle asked as she tossed the brush back into the bucket. She turned, crossing her arms over her chest. "Is she part of your harem of women who bow at your every command?"

Colt burst out laughing. He couldn't help himself. Damn if Annabelle Carter wasn't a good time. He could almost be her friend if business and his hormones weren't in the way.

"Winnie is actually my cook, but she'll get a kick out of your guess."

Annabelle eyed the basket, then narrowed her eyes back on him. "Why did she do that? I can make my own dinner."

"You can," he agreed. "But you were exhausted when you left here yesterday and still had to go home and cook. Then I heard you tell your dad you were up at four this morning to feed Emily and I'm sure you were up with Lucy, as well. No reason I can't make your situation a little easier."

He wasn't sure what reaction he expected her to have, but when she threw her arms in the air and turned to pace, he waited. If nothing else, the woman always kept him on his toes.

"You can't do things like this," she all but shouted

as she whirled back around. "I'm trying to hate you, to remind myself that you're the enemy. But part of me wants to believe you're not a monster and when all is said and done, I won't get hurt."

Guilt slid through him, but he couldn't let it hinder his plans. He still had a goal. But damn it, Annabelle touched something in him that he couldn't identify and he had no clue how he could make the outcome less painful for her. There was no happy ending.

Still, she made it impossible not to like her. She made him want to go the extra mile to make her days easier and ignore the inevitable pain he would cause.

Life was so much easier when Colt was only dealing with Neil.

"But you do things like this and I don't know what angle you're working," she went on, her tone lowering as she seemed to be running out of steam. As she spoke, he advanced, step by slow step. "If you're trying to seduce me, I can tell you you're wasting your time. Even if I find you attractive, that doesn't matter. I can't—"

Colt gripped her shoulders, backing her up to the post between the stalls. "You find me attractive?"

Her lids closed as she blew out a breath. "That is all you would take away from what I said."

How could he not? He was going to take this minor victory and run with it. Not that he hadn't already guessed it, but to hear her admit her thoughts had his body tightening.

Colt knew he'd have to take advantage of every moment of her weakness if he wanted to penetrate that wall of defense she'd erected.

He leaned in closer as he flattened his palms on either side of her head. Her flush from the work she'd done, her musky scent, the way her chest rose and fell against his own, it would be so easy to turn this into something more right here and now. They were alone, there was nothing stopping him. And he knew Annabelle was his for the taking.

Colt shifted until his lips grazed across hers like a whisper. "A man could get used to hearing a beautiful woman give him compliments."

"Then maybe you should find a beautiful woman who wants to," she murmured.

He nipped at her bottom lip. "I've found her."

"Colt." Her hands came up to his chest.

The way his name came out on a breathy sigh had his entire body stirring to life. The fight she attempted to put up was weak. There was no conviction in her tone, no pressure from her hands to push him away.

How could he want someone so desperately? He had always been able to control his needs, but not with Annabelle. She challenged him in so many ways, and she was the one woman he really shouldn't want.

Still, seducing her was too sweet, too perfect.

Keeping one hand beside her face, he ran the other over her hip. His thumb slid beneath the hem of her tank. Her smooth skin beneath his touch was everything he'd been dreaming of…and he'd dreamt of her plenty last night.

"I want you."

"No, you want to control me."

"Only in bed."

Her eyes met his. "You're blunt."

"Honest," he corrected, going in to graze her lips once again.

"You have no idea what you're doing," she muttered, as if thinking out loud. "I'm not… Trust me when I say you don't want me."

He cupped her cheek with one hand, his other still at her hip. "Don't put yourself down. I know exactly what I want and I assure you, it's you."

"I'm not putting myself down or fishing for compliments. But you need to know that I'm…"

"What?" he urged.

Now she did push him away. "Not for you."

She picked up the basket, keeping her back to him. Shoulders hunched, she appeared to be defeated. How was that possible? His body was revved up and she seemed as if she'd just lost a battle. They could both win here if she'd just quit fighting the chemistry.

"Just take me home," she whispered. "I can't do this."

When he didn't make a move, she turned to face him, tears swimming in her eyes. "Please."

Whatever internal battle she waged with herself, Colt wanted no part of it. He'd wanted simple, he'd wanted sex. He still did.

Someone like Annabelle would take time to seduce, but he wasn't about to back down. She was needy, aching, just the same as him. He'd felt her heart beat against his chest, felt her arch into him slightly before she pushed him away.

It was only a matter of time before he unleashed that passion.

* * *

Annabelle's hands still shook as she unloaded the basket.

Get a grip.

She tried to focus on the amazing food that Colt's cook had prepared. The fact he'd done this for her simply because he'd heard her discuss her hectic home life… Annabelle had no words to describe her emotions.

Of course, maybe she was speechless because her brain was totally fried after that heated encounter in the barn. Yet as hands-on and blatantly sexual as he'd been, he was a total gentleman on the ride home—in his truck. He'd also procured a bag of dog food for the new pup. Confusing, frustrating man. And she'd never wanted anyone more.

"What's all this?"

Her father stood in the doorway, holding Emily and patting her back.

"Dinner. Where is Lucy?"

"She's content chewing a doll head in the Pack 'n Play. I actually just fed her some apricots." He eased Emily into one of two high chairs. "Where on earth did you get all of that food?"

"Colt's cook made extra."

She didn't look up as she busied herself unwrapping everything. No way did she want to see her father's face. She already knew she'd have to answer questions.

"Colt's cook, huh? Sounds like you're getting friendly with him."

Friendly wasn't the correct term. But she truly didn't know what label to give this warped situation. She was caught in between the proverbial rock and a hard place, all the while getting completely turned on by her boss.

Of all the men she could feel a stirring for, why did Colt Elliott have to be the one? She hated her emotions, but the reality was, she felt more of a need, an ache for Colt than she ever did with Matt, and they'd been engaged.

In light of all that had happened, though, Annabelle was relieved she hadn't slept with Matt, that he'd respected her wishes to wait until they were married.

But if the scenario were different and she were engaged to Colt, she couldn't guarantee she'd wait.

"Belle?" Her father waved a hand in front of her face. "What the hell is going on? You bring home this food, you're daydreaming. Is that Elliott boy pressuring you?"

Boy? Not hardly. Colt was all man.

Annabelle circled the long farm-style table and crossed to the high chair. Emily's big green eyes met hers and Annabelle's heart melted. She loved her girls so much. Even though her sister had betrayed her in an unforgivable way, they'd still been family and these twins were all Annabelle had left.

She kissed Emily on her head, smoothing the red curls aside. "He's my temporary boss, Dad. Nothing more."

That wasn't a lie, not for lack of trying on Colt's part, but it was clearly a tidbit of information her father didn't need to know about. That kiss out in the field had to remain her secret…and her fantasy.

Emily clapped her hands together, then banged them on the tray. "How has her fever been today?"

"Just a little this morning, but otherwise it hasn't come back. She's played more this afternoon."

Annabelle went to the pantry and pulled out a jar of baby food. "Never worry about calling me. I want to know if there's any problem with her or you."

Neil grabbed two plates from the cupboard and started filling them with homemade fried chicken, mashed potatoes, and corn. The homemade rolls had Annabelle salivating. She'd hurried through her glamorous lunch of a turkey sandwich so she could get back to work. Ranching was the fastest way she'd ever known to burn calories.

"Where's the puppy?" she asked, glancing around the kitchen.

"I put him outside in the fenced area to run around for a bit. He's a cute little guy, but a handful when I'm alone with the two girls."

Annabelle couldn't feel guilty about that. The situation they were in was part his fault, part fate.

As far as the dog was concerned, she should come up with a name for him soon. She wished the girls were old enough to decide, but at six months, they were just making random sounds and squealing.

Annabelle pulled a wooden kitchen chair over to the high chair and scooped up a bite from the jar. Emily pressed her lips together and turned her head.

"If that's green beans, I tried those for lunch. She hates them. Though Lucy was quite a fan. They're total opposites, except for their looks."

Annabelle chased Emily's mouth around with the spoon. "Yeah, well, I'd like a chocolate cake for dinner, too, but we can't all have that. Come on, little one. Veggies are good."

As she wrestled bite after bite past Emily's lips, Annabelle went over in her head exactly how to approach her father about the debt to Colt's family. It was more than the house, she was positive. Colt, surprisingly, hadn't been willing to throw her dad under the bus. But she needed to know what she was up against. She didn't have time to try to piece all these snippets together for the full story.

Maybe being blunt was the best approach. "Did you gamble against Colt's father before all of this happened?"

"What?" he asked, his fork clanging against his plate.

Annabelle shifted in her seat to face him. "Before now, had you borrowed money or gambled against Colt's father?"

Neil Carter's face tightened, his lips thinned. "Is that what he told you?"

Attempting to distract herself from the ball of tension in her stomach, Annabelle scooped up another bite for Emily. "He didn't tell me anything. That's why I'm asking you."

"There's nothing for you to worry about." He aggressively cut into his chicken. "I don't like you working over there, Belle. You and I can move and start over. We don't have to stay here, you know."

Nearly everything she'd ever loved had been taken from her and as long as there was fight left in her and a chance this place could be hers again, she wouldn't back down.

"If you want to go, then go."

She knew he could never afford to live on his own. His addiction wouldn't allow it. He didn't have any savings, and everything she was bringing in would have to go to bills. There was no extra.

"We can find something inexpensive," he argued. "I know your mother had this dream, but she's gone and…"

"Well, I'm still here," she snapped. "I will see this through with or without your help."

Her father leaned back in his seat and raked a hand down his face. "Don't let them come between us. You've been over there for two days and your attitude has changed already."

Perhaps she had changed, but not because of Colt.

"I'm not the same person I was a month ago," she informed him. She scraped the bottom of the jar and fought to get the last bite into Emily's mouth. "Losing my sister and fiancé, then finding out they were having an affair pretty much destroyed me."

"I lost a daughter," he murmured. "I know how much it hurts."

Yes, he was hurting, too. But, they were both feeling different types of pain. He'd lost a child, Annabelle had lost her future. They were going to have to lean on each other to get through this nightmare or she'd never make it.

"I need you here," she told him. "I need you for Emily and Lucy so I can work. You need to get better for not just yourself, but for those babies who will look up to you one day. And I need you to work on making yourself the father I used to know because I can't do this without him."

Her voice caught on that last word. Tears clogged her throat as she blinked away moisture. Sometimes a girl just needed her dad.

"I'm trying."

Silence settled between them. Suddenly she wasn't in the mood to eat. She pulled Emily from the high chair and wiped her mouth with the bib before tugging it over her head. She dropped the dirty rag onto the tray.

"I'm going to give her a bath and then I'll come back for Lucy," Annabelle told her father. "If you can let the dog in and feed him, that would be great. I'll clean the kitchen later, after the girls are bathed."

"You're not eating?" he asked as she headed out of the room.

"I'm fine," she lied. But she didn't want to get into the mess inside her head. Especially not with her father.

Annabelle hugged Emily a bit tighter as she mounted the steps. "We're going to make it," she vowed. "You guys will have a stable home and never doubt my love. We're in this together."

All Annabelle had to do was make it through the next three months and she'd be free. She'd be able to push forward, take control of her life once and for all…and be rid of Colt Elliott.

Eight

"Hayes will be home next month."

Nolan laid the blanket across the horse he'd appropriately named Doc. Colt grabbed his own blanket and saddle and readied his stallion.

"I already asked Charlie to get the house ready and stock it before he arrives," Colt replied. "I'm sure he'll be ready to have some downtime to adjust to civilian life again."

Hayes had been in the service for the past fifteen years. He'd enlisted straight out of high school and now he was getting out for good. They'd thought he'd stay in a few more years and then retire, but Hayes wasn't the same man he used to be. He'd seen too much, things he'd never discuss, and there had been a haunted look in his eyes last time he'd been home.

Colt wasn't sure if Hayes would want anything to do with ranch life or if he'd like to explore other venues, but Colt would readily welcome him here for as long as he wanted to stay. Hayes had enough money that he'd never have to work a day in his life, but Colt intended to keep him a little busy so those demons didn't creep up and take control.

"Think Dad will remember him?" Colt asked.

Nolan hoisted the saddle across his stallion's back. "Depends on the day Hayes goes to see him. I stopped in earlier after my shift and he wasn't having the best day. He kept telling me to find Virginia because the dog had been hit by a car."

Virginia, their mother, had been gone for years. He still asked about her, still would question why she wasn't there. He may have dementia, but they had a love that would rival any fairy tale Colt had ever heard.

"That dog was killed when I was a baby," Nolan added. "So he's gone back pretty far. He thought I was Hank."

Hank had been their father's right-hand man at the stables, but he, too, had passed on. Their father was a prisoner in his own mind and he had no clue. All they could do was keep visiting, and hopefully he could grasp that he wasn't alone in his living hell.

"I'm going to see him tomorrow." Colt adjusted the saddle and patted Lightning's side before mounting him. "It's been a hectic couple of days."

When Annabelle had gone home an hour ago, Colt had been too keyed up to do anything. He'd just wanted to ride, but then Nolan had stopped in for some downtime.

"How's your new employee working out?" Nolan asked as he set off toward the back pasture.

Colt gripped the reins in one hand and tipped his hat down with the other. Who knew what truth his eyes would tell? He'd thought of little else since that kiss. Well, he'd thought of excuses to touch her again, because he was having a damn hard time *not* touching her.

"She's a hard worker. Josh and Ryan are impressed, too."

He rode parallel with Nolan, as they'd done so many times over the years. The inquisition was coming, Colt would bet the ranch on it.

"And you?" Nolan asked easily. "You're impressed."

He could still feel her tight body against his when he'd pressed her against the wall. Could still feel that warm breath brush across his cheek, his neck. She wasn't immune to their chemistry. She practically melted against him when they touched, and he couldn't wait until she was his.

"She doesn't complain about the heat or the work. She does her job and is prompt."

The sun, barely visible on the horizon now, cast an orange glow. The gorgeous summer nights never ceased to catch his breath. There was nothing more peaceful than a sunset on the ranch. There was nowhere else he'd rather spend his days than Pebblebrook.

"This is a hard life," Nolan said, giving Doc a gentle pat. "Think she'll be just as professional in three months?"

"She's determined to pay off her father's debt. She knows I want her land."

Nolan's disapproving sigh had Colt gritting his teeth. "Don't start," Colt warned.

"I didn't say a word. Sounds like the guilt is already getting to you."

That wasn't the only thing getting to him.

"I can't make decisions based on personal feelings, Nolan. This ranch is a business."

"Fair enough. So what are you going to do at the end of this, when the debt is paid?"

Colt rubbed the back of his neck. "I'm going to give them time to find another place."

"She's not going to be happy."

Colt pulled Lightning to a stop. "I'm not making friends. I'm pursuing a goal Dad had and I'm making sure it's carried out. How do you suggest I acquire the land? Because I asked multiple times to buy it."

Nolan eased to a standstill as well and glanced around at the acreage stretching as far as the eye could see. "You know, I made a poor choice years ago that affected the rest of my life. I just don't want to see you doing something you regret."

Colt didn't need his oldest brother to spell out the mistake he'd made. Nolan had been in love, but when she'd pressured him to settle down, he'd gotten scared. Add an unexpected pregnancy and a miscarriage and Nolan hadn't been able to deal.

While Colt didn't know the entire story, he knew Nolan had never found that type of bond since. He flitted between the hospital and dates, occasionally working on the ranch when he could. But there was barely a weekend that Nolan didn't have someone on his arm...

or in his bed. Of course, he never brought women back to Pebblebrook because that would be too personal.

"I'd regret if I let that land go," Colt stated simply. "I'm going to turn Pebblebrook into the greatest dude ranch the west has ever seen. I already have an engineer coming to draw up some plans for renovations on the house next door."

Nolan tugged his hat off and settled it onto the horn. "I wouldn't let Annabelle know that."

"She doesn't."

His brother's blue eyes bore into Colt. "You're starting to care for her. What are you going to do when you can't stop your feelings from getting involved with business?"

Colt snorted. "I want to take her to bed, if that's what you mean by 'care for her.' You should know something about meaningless sex."

Nolan nodded. "Touché."

"Besides, I want to settle down eventually. I definitely want kids to fill Pebblebrook with, but I want my dude ranch and my life in order first."

Laughing, Nolan shook his head. "There's no perfect time to start a family and settle down. You need to do it when you find the one or you'll be left alone, trying to fill a void you caused."

Colt wasn't worried he'd fall for Annabelle. They wanted vastly different things and just because he ached to strip her down and have his way with her, didn't mean he was ready to monogram her initials on the plush towels in his master bath.

Tugging on his reins once more, Colt settled into an

easy pace. "I've got a rancher from Oklahoma coming in two days to pick up forty head of cattle."

"Can't help you there. I'm on call for the next three days, starting tomorrow."

"Weren't you just on call?" Colt asked.

Nolan's horse jerked to the side before Nolan eased him back. "I was, but I picked up some extra shifts for a coworker. He's taking his wife on a surprise second honeymoon."

"You're going to work yourself to death."

Nolan cast a sideways glance. "I could say the same for you. But we're doing what we love, so it doesn't feel like work."

There was nothing else Colt had ever wanted to do. Nothing could pull him from Pebblebrook. He was anxious to have Hayes come back, and maybe he could help out for a bit until he decided fully what he wanted to do. Beau had been filming a movie in parts unknown for the past few months. Some action film where he would surely win the lady and save the day.

"Storms are coming in," Nolan stated, nodding toward the darkening skies.

Colt pulled on the reins. "We'll head back."

Colt couldn't recall the last time all four of them were together, but he was definitely going to call Beau and see if he could fly home for Hayes's homecoming. Maybe they could even all go visit their father. Better yet, maybe they could bring him to the ranch for a day.

Emotions threatened to overtake him at the idea of all of them there once again. Colt may be the youngest, but he had the most to prove. He wanted this property

to thrive bigger and better than it ever had. He wanted
his brothers to see just how hard he worked to make
sure Pebblebrook remained the greatest ranch in Texas.
And even though his father didn't always know what
was going on in the world around him, Colt was going
to honor him and personally see to it that his dude ranch
came to fruition.

He'd set this dream in motion, so failing now would
be a sure sign that he couldn't handle tough times. There
was no way he'd let this scenario end without him getting the land and the house.

And letting Annabelle Carter appeal to his compas-
sionate side was not an option. The only place he wanted
her was in his bed.

"The truck?" Annabelle asked as she climbed into
the cab. She set the basket from last night between them
and reached for her seat belt. "Did I get a promotion?"

Colt dangled his wrist over the steering wheel and
shot her a smile that shot straight to her heart. The instant response wasn't welcome, but she had no way of
stopping it. At this point, all she could do was hang on
for the ride.

"I need to run into town real quick and thought you'd
enjoy a few minutes of air-conditioning before we hit
it hard today."

Annabelle stretched her denim-covered legs out.
"You're the boss."

"I do like how you keep saying that, sweets."

She let out a groan. "*Ms. Carter* still works fine."

Tipping his hat, he pinned her with his striking gaze.

"You've arched that sweet body against mine, you've kissed me, and you've imagined us as lovers. We're beyond formalities."

Annabelle's breath caught in her throat. She'd never met a man so blunt…and so dead-on with calling her out on her feelings. But she was a different woman than she was even a month ago and she wasn't about to be intimidated by Colt Elliott.

"That may be," she stated as she leaned closer, pleased when his eyes dropped to her lips. "But you've had the same thoughts, and you're no closer to getting me there than you were days ago."

Colt reached out, curling his fingers around the back of her neck. He captured her mouth, parting her lips, tangling his tongue with hers. The intensity of his touch, the urgency of the demanding kiss should have scared her, but Annabelle was too turned-on, too stunned at his actions to be frightened.

This was nothing like the sweet, delicate kiss he'd first given her. This was a toe-curling, body-tingling kiss like nothing she'd ever experienced before.

Annabelle fisted her hands in her lap, refusing to reach for him…but she wasn't going to deny she didn't want this to end.

Colt's grip on her neck softened as he trailed his fingers around to her jaw. Gently, he nipped at her lips before easing back. He stroked the pad of his thumb across her bottom lip and Annabelle couldn't stop her tongue from darting out and tasting him.

"I'd say we're one step closer," he murmured.

Annabelle was just digesting those words when he

pulled back and reached over to start the truck. She had a snappy comeback, something snarky about his arrogance taking place of his ego, but when he extended his arm and waved, Annabelle cringed. She turned to see her father standing on the porch, cradling a girl on each hip, and from the look of his face, he'd witnessed everything.

Great. Nothing like having your father see you make out with the enemy. Just when she thought this situation couldn't get any worse.

Nine

At the end of the day Colt was still cursing himself for losing control with Annabelle earlier. Not that he regretted finally getting to taste those sweet lips again. No, he was more irritated with himself than the fact that he'd let her goad him. He did everything on his terms, his timeline.

The kicker had been looking up and seeing Neil on the porch, holding Emily and Lucy, that pup frolicking around his feet. Colt didn't mind that her father had seen them because he honestly didn't care what the old man thought. But he sure as hell didn't want an audience when his seduction of Annabelle was finally complete. He wanted to get her alone, to prove to her that they were indeed closer to intimacy. They'd been dancing around the subject for days and it was only a matter of time before they succumbed to what they both wanted. There was no way she could deny that, not after the way she kept responding to his kisses.

Colt had put Annabelle with Ryan today because he'd needed some time to think. When he was around her, he felt his control slipping by the second. He still had a ranch to run, and besides, he'd wanted to sneak away to visit his father.

Today had not been a good day for Grant Elliott. He hadn't recognized Colt at all. No matter what happened in Colt's life, nothing hurt more than looking into his father's blue eyes and seeing the blank stare, the confusion.

But his father had talked about a dude ranch. Colt had listened as his dad went on about all the things he'd incorporate onto the farm. The small cabins he'd build on the east side where the view of the pasture was breathtaking at sunset, the horses he'd bring in special for children who came to visit. He'd even mentioned having programs for physically handicapped riders who wanted to see what ranching was all about.

Colt knew his father was in there somewhere because he'd mentioned all of his original plans. Ranching had been so ingrained into the Elliott patriarch, that it was something Colt didn't think would ever be lost to this nightmare disease.

He had asked the nursing staff about the possibility of bringing his father home for one day when Hayes returned but, in the end, they decided to play it by ear. As much as Colt wanted his father at Pebblebrook, even for a short time, he would do whatever was best for his health.

Colt shut off the engine and grabbed his hat from the passenger seat. As he stepped from his truck, Colt headed toward the barn, but froze for a split second before taking off in a dead run. Annabelle lay on the ground just inside the structure, Ryan kneeling over her and patting the side of her face.

"What the hell happened?" Colt asked, skidding to a stop and dropping to his knees.

"She passed out, Boss."

Her color was off, perspiration dotted her forehead. He glanced at her body and noted that the white tank she'd worn was clinging to the dampness on her torso. He jerked his hat off and started to fan her.

"Get some water," Colt demanded, never taking his eyes off her pale face. He felt the pulse on her neck. Steady, thankfully, but he didn't like seeing her on the damn ground.

While Ryan rushed to the office, Colt eased his arms beneath her knees and her back. Carefully, he lifted her and stepped back to take a seat on a bench. Her lids fluttered as her head fell toward his chest. Ryan came back with a bottle of water and handed it to Colt.

"Want me to call Nolan?" Ryan asked.

Colt shook his head. "He's at the hospital. She's coming around."

Slowly, she turned her head, her brows dipping as if she was hurt. "What happened?" Colt asked again. "Were you in here when she fainted? Where's Josh?"

"Josh took off early because his daughter has some

dance recital." Ryan pulled a handkerchief from his back pocket and wiped the back of his neck. "Ms. Carter and I had been out herding the cattle from the west field and we'd just gotten back. I walked around the side to turn the hoses on and when I came back in, she was all flushed. I asked if she felt all right, but she went down. I was fast enough to catch her before she hit her head, though. Scared ten years off my life."

Yeah, Colt was still trying to get his heart rate back under control after seeing her motionless on the ground.

"What else should I do?"

Colt shook his head and focused back on Annabelle. "I'd say she got overheated. It happens. Why don't you go ahead and tend to the horses and get them put away? I'll take care of her."

Ryan gave a clipped nod. "Yell if you need me."

Cradling her with one arm, Colt set the water bottle on the bench beside him and smoothed the stray, damp tendrils from her face. Her lids fluttered again and he silently pleaded for her to open them and give him hell for holding her.

He'd seen many cowboys go down due to heat and lack of hydration, but none of them had affected him like this. She'd worked herself to the point of exhaustion, and it was all his fault.

"Open those eyes, sweetness."

She fluttered once again. "You never ask nice," she murmured.

Relief spread through him as swiftly as a Texas storm in the spring.

Finally, those bright green eyes met his and for the first time in several minutes, he breathed a sigh of relief.

"Wh-what are you doing?" she asked, starting to ease up.

"Stay still." Damn it, he needed to hold her another minute. "You passed out."

One shaky hand came up to her forehead as she blinked in confusion. "I did? Where's Ryan? We were going to—"

"Forget it. He's outside tending to the horses and you're done for the day."

He helped her sit up, but kept a hold around her shoulders. Colt reached for the water bottle and brought it to her lips. "Drink."

She took the water from him and sipped, then swiped the bottle across her forehead. Condensation slid down the side of her face, down her neck, and disappeared into the scoop of her tank. He shouldn't be thinking how sexy she looked right now, but he couldn't help himself. He'd been away from her all day, then to come back and see this…his emotions were in overdrive.

"You have to take care of yourself," he stated, his tone much harsher than he'd intended.

With careful movements, she slid from his lap and set the bottle down on the bench. "My welfare is none of your concern. I take care of myself just fine."

He came to his feet, going toe to toe with her. "Clearly not. And your welfare is my concern when it affects your work."

When she squared her shoulders, but rubbed her forehead as if her head ached, he felt like an ass. She was gearing up for a fight and he was just angry he hadn't been there to make sure she was fine.

"Damn it." He raked a hand down his face. "Get in the truck, I'll take you home."

"I'll ask Ryan."

Colt leaned forward, towering over her until she reached for his shoulders to stay upright. "When you need anything, I'll be the one to deliver it. Get. In. The. Truck."

Her eyes searched his face. "Something happened."

"Yeah, you passed out and scared the hell out of us."

She shook her head, her hands softened against him. "Something else. You're angry at me, but there's a sadness in your eyes I haven't seen before."

Colt hated how she homed directly in on the nugget inside him he tried so damn hard to keep hidden from the world. "Don't analyze me, sweetness. Unless you want to get into *your* secrets."

"I just thought…" She took a step away and swiped the back of her hand across her forehead. "Nothing. Forget I asked."

When she turned to head toward the truck, Colt grabbed her arm and hauled her side against his chest. "I had a bad day. That's all. It's nothing I want to talk about, but, thanks. I've never met anyone who knows what I'm feeling or thinking without me saying a word."

Those captivating eyes turned to him. "Maybe one broken heart recognizes another."

"Who broke your heart?" he whispered.

Her eyes went to his throat, as if she couldn't look directly at him. "Who hasn't?"

Those two words spoke volumes. She'd been broken, perhaps she still was, but she was a damn fighter. She stood before him ready to discuss what pained him when she was clearly just as shattered. But he wasn't asking, he couldn't. Getting involved on an emotional level was not an option. How many times did he have to remind himself of that?

Colt gripped her chin between his thumb and finger, tipping her head to capture her lips. Softly he caressed her mouth with his. His knees weakened the second she slid her hand over his forearm. The kiss was so innocent, definitely not the stepping-stone to sex he typically delivered. But this was the most relaxed he'd ever known her to be. Her body literally eased against his as she returned the passion so delicately.

"Maybe someday you'll trust me," he muttered against her lips.

Her hand tightened against him. "It's not my trust you're after."

Colt grazed her lips once again. "Maybe not, but if you trust me, then you'll be more likely to give me everything else I want from you."

Annabelle eased away as she blew out a sigh. "We both know that would be a terrible idea. I've still got months to go and we're already…"

"What are we? Because this could be so much better."

She glanced out the doorway. With the light breeze blowing in, strands from her ponytail danced around her shoulders. "I can't get involved with you, Colt. I already have to explain this morning's kiss to my father when I get home."

"You didn't go home for lunch?" he asked.

She shook her head. "I couldn't face him. After all that's happened—"

"Nothing has happened."

She turned her attention back to him. "Yet, right? You fully intend to keep this up until I give in."

Why answer such a rhetorical question? They both knew what was going on, they were adults. Colt wanted Annabelle and the feeling was mutual. He knew desire when it stared back at him.

"Come up to the house."

Those green eyes widened. "What?"

"For dinner. We'll talk." He held his hands out. "Nothing more. I swear."

Unless she wanted more, then who would he be to turn her down?

"I need to get home to the girls."

"Bring them."

What the hell was he saying? He never dated a woman with a baby, let alone twins. Never brought kids back to his home. But why shouldn't he now? It was no secret that he wanted Annabelle. Perhaps appealing to that side of her would make her come around.

Annabelle laughed. "Wow. You're letting your desperation show, Colt."

Yeah, maybe he was, but he wanted her trust, damn it. He was running out of patience. His body ached for her, responded to her when she merely cast a glance his way. He'd never felt this urgency toward one woman before.

"Give your dad the night off and bring your twins to the house. I know Winnie will have a feast prepared. She always does."

He could see her thinking, but refused to take no for an answer. "One dinner, darlin'. That's all. I think you could use a break."

"Fine," she sighed. "I'll bring Emily and Lucy in my own car and you will not touch me. Deal?"

Colt winked. "Sure thing, but what happens when you touch me?"

With an unladylike growl, she spun around and headed out the barn. "In your dreams."

"Every damn night," he muttered to her retreating back.

Ten

"You're not seriously going over there."

Annabelle slipped on her flip-flops and picked Emily up. "I'm only going for dinner. Anything I can do to stay on his good side and figure out his ulterior motive, I'll do it."

"I saw you doing it in his truck this morning."

The accusing tone, the knowing glare had guilt surging through Annabelle. She'd been home for nearly thirty minutes, long enough to change clothes and feed the girls, before he said anything. But she refused to allow him to turn this around on her.

"You're the reason I'm in this position," she countered, keeping her tone light since she held Emily.

"That's your excuse for kissing Colt Elliott?" Her father's silver brows drew in as he crossed his arms over his chest. "That man doesn't care about you, Belle. People like the Elliotts only care about money."

She swallowed back the hurt. Someday a man would be interested in her for no other reason than the fact that he liked, or even loved her. She'd been used and discarded too many times to care right now, though. Kissing Colt had been a pleasure, and she was going to steal those moments when she could. She was smart enough to know Colt wanted her in bed. And she couldn't deny she'd been fantasizing about it.

"Leave the girls here," her father stated.

Annabelle shook her head. She needed them as the buffer. "We'll be fine. Besides, I don't get to see them much."

"At least leave Emily since she's still been fussing."

"I'll take Lucy," she stated. She had to drive home to Colt that she wasn't the type to play around. She had a family she needed to look out for.

Finally, her father nodded. "I'm going to need some cash."

"What for?"

She'd taken over all finances, cutting him off since she'd been back. Until he proved himself to be addiction free, it was the only way for them to get his debt paid off in time.

"I'll go to the grocery while you're gone. We're low on diapers and we could use some milk and eggs."

Annabelle did the quick math in her head. Holding Emily on her hip, she crossed to her purse hanging by the front door. She pulled out a few bills and handed them to her father.

"Just put the change back in my purse," she told him. "I shouldn't be too long."

Before he could make another argument as to why she shouldn't go, Annabelle grabbed the diaper bag and her keys and headed out the door. Once she got to Pebblebrook, she pulled in to the large, circular drive near the front door. She'd only been in his office, so she had to admit she was curious about what the rest of the house looked like. Did any other rooms have that spectacular waterfall?

Annabelle unfastened Lucy from her car seat and headed up the wide stone steps. The small creek running in front of the home soothed her nerves with the trickling effect. She knew coming here was just another tactic of Colt's to sway her into his bed. Little did he know nobody had been able to accomplish that in the past and she had a strong resolve built up. Well, she couldn't deny it was slipping, but she could hold out longer than him.

And she was pretty confident she was driving him insane. He wanted her and he was getting desperate. A thrill of power shot through her.

When the wide door swung open just as she hit the top step, Annabelle was a little surprised to see Colt in the entryway.

"I figured one of your minions would answer the door."

He held a hand over his heart and stepped aside for her to enter. "I'm crushed you think so little of me."

"You think enough of yourself for both of us," she countered as she stepped over the threshold.

Dear Reader,

IT'S A FACT: if you answer 4 quick questions, we'll send you **4 FREE REWARDS!**

I'm not kidding you. As a leading publisher of women's fiction, we value your opinions... and your time. That's why we are prepared to **reward** you handsomely for completing our mini-survey. In fact, we have 4 Free Rewards for you, including 2 free books and 2 free gifts.

As you may have guessed, that's why our mini-survey is called **"4 for 4".** Answer 4 questions and get 4 Free Rewards. It's that simple!

Thank you for participating in our survey,

Pam Powers

To get your 4 FREE REWARDS:
Complete the survey below and return the insert today to receive 2 FREE BOOKS and 2 FREE GIFTS guaranteed!

► DETACH AND MAIL CARD TODAY! ►

"4 for 4" MINI-SURVEY

1 Is reading one of your favorite hobbies?
☐ YES   ☐ NO

2 Do you prefer to read instead of watch TV?
☐ YES   ☐ NO

3 Do you read newspapers and magazines?
☐ YES   ☐ NO

4 Do you enjoy trying new book series with FREE BOOKS?
☐ YES   ☐ NO

YES! I have completed the above Mini-Survey. Please send me my 4 FREE REWARDS (worth over $20 retail). I understand that I am under no obligation to buy anything, as explained on the back of this card.

225/326 HDL GLPL

FIRST NAME _____   LAST NAME _____

ADDRESS _____

APT.# _____   CITY _____

STATE/PROV. _____   ZIP/POSTAL CODE _____

READER SERVICE—Here's how it works:

Accepting your 2 free Harlequin Desire® books and 2 free gifts (gifts valued at approximately $10.00) places you under no obligation to buy anything. You may keep the books and gifts and return the shipping statement marked "cancel." If you do not cancel, about a month later we'll send you 6 additional books and bill you just $4.80 each in the U.S. or $5.49 each in Canada. That is a savings of at least 8% off the cover price. It's quite a bargain! Shipping and handling is just 50¢ per book in the U.S. and 75¢ per book in Canada.* You may cancel at any time, but if you choose to continue, every month we'll send you 6 more books, which you may either purchase at the discount price plus shipping and handling or return to us and cancel your subscription. *Terms and prices subject to change without notice. Prices do not include applicable taxes. Sales tax applicable in N.Y. Canadian residents will be charged applicable taxes. Offer not valid in Quebec. Books received may not be as shown. All orders subject to approval. Credit or debit balances in a customer's account(s) may be offset by any other outstanding balance owed by or to the customer. Please allow 4 to 6 weeks for delivery. Offer available while quantities last.

◀ If offer card is missing write to: Reader Service, P.O. Box 1867, Buffalo, NY 14240-1867 or visit www.ReaderService.com ◀

BUSINESS REPLY MAIL
FIRST-CLASS MAIL   PERMIT NO. 717   BUFFALO, NY

POSTAGE WILL BE PAID BY ADDRESSEE

READER SERVICE
PO BOX 1867
BUFFALO NY 14240-9952

NO POSTAGE
NECESSARY
IF MAILED
IN THE
UNITED STATES

The house was just as gorgeous as she remembered. Breathtaking. So far out of her league, she was afraid to take a step any farther. But she took her time in glancing around, taking it all in.

"Just one of the girls?" he asked.

Annabelle nodded. "This is Lucy. Emily stayed with my dad. I won't know how to act with just one. I'm always taking care of them both at the same time."

"Let me have the bag." Colt eased the diaper bag off her shoulder and set it on the accent table next to an enormous vase containing a spray of bright flowers. "Follow me. Winnie did indeed make a feast and she was thrilled to have someone enjoy it other than me."

"Where is she?"

"Oh, she's probably heading home," he replied as he led her down the wide hallway toward the back of the house. "She went to her suite earlier, but she's not staying."

Her suite. Of course. What chef didn't have their own suite?

Annabelle held on tight to Lucy, who had finally laid her head down on Annabelle's shoulder. It had been a long day for everyone.

"How are you feeling?" Colt asked, stepping into the massive kitchen.

"I'm fine." Even if she weren't, she wouldn't admit it. She was still mortified she'd passed out earlier. But, the moment she'd woken up, she'd seen that worry on Colt's face. That was definitely something he couldn't fake.

Annabelle tried not to gawk, but she couldn't help herself. The massive center island dominated the kitchen. It featured a small sink and a second gas stove as well as an overhang stretching across the length of the island. There were even bar stools made from antique saddles.

Massive dishes of food had been set out: cornbread, potatoes, smoked sausages with peppers, and a pie. Apple. Her favorite. The spread on the island had her mouth watering.

"I should've worn my bigger jeans." Her stomach growled and she cringed. "And I shouldn't have skipped lunch."

His bright eyes narrowed. "No, you shouldn't have. You know how hard ranch work is and you need to take care of yourself."

Annabelle nodded. "It won't happen again. Believe me." Lucy let out a deep sigh. "I'm pretty sure she's fallen asleep."

Annabelle turned so the baby faced Colt. "Is she?"

"Oh, yeah. She's out."

Grabbing a plate off the edge of the bar, Annabelle started dishing up potatoes with one hand.

"I'll get your damn plate."

She eyed him. "No language around the baby."

Tipping his head, he pursed his lips. "She's already talking?"

"Well, no, but I don't want *damn* to be her first word, either."

"Fair enough, sweetness."

Rolling her eyes, she set her plate down and glared at him. "You've got to stop with the tacky pet names.

I'm sure you've used those names on a number of other women, but I'm not falling for your charms."

"You think I'm charming?" That sidelong grin had her body instantly responding. "And I've never used *sweetness* on anyone else. Maybe that can be your name."

Slowly easing Lucy to her other side, Annabelle snorted. "I'd rather you not call me that, especially when we're working."

He put a piece of cornbread on the side of her plate and turned to face her, pinning her with that direct baby-blue gaze. "And when we're not working?"

She would not stand there and flirt with him. She had to cut that off before it could get started because she was losing ground. Her willpower was cracking and she couldn't afford to have it completely crumble.

Breaking his stare, Annabelle turned away. She headed toward the long, farm-style table in front of the floor-to-ceiling windows looking out onto the pool. Of course there was a pool house off to the side. She could only imagine what that looked like inside.

"Good evening." Annabelle jerked toward the doorway to see a beaming elderly woman. "I'm Winnie. I won't get in the way, I just wanted to introduce myself and tell you how amazing that cinnamon bread you sent back was."

Annabelle ignored the way Colt's gaze widened. "You're welcome. I love to bake and wanted to thank you for the dinner. I guess I should be thanking you for two."

She waved a hand. "It's no trouble at all. I'm happy

to have someone else to cook for. I'd love for you to share that recipe, if you don't mind."

"I don't mind a bit," Annabelle replied with a smile.

"You made bread?" Colt finally asked as he poured two glasses of sweet tea.

"It was in the basket she sent back," Winnie stated.

"I had no idea or I would've dug into it." Colt crossed the kitchen and set Annabelle's plate and tea on the table. "This looks delicious, as always, Winnie. Did you eat?"

"I did." Her eyes zeroed in on Emily. "And who is this precious baby?"

"My daughter, Lucy." That still felt so strange to say. There were so many emotions tied to the fact the twins were legally hers. Emotions she'd not fully faced. "She and her twin, Lucy, are six months old."

"Oh, my. Two precious angels. Well, she's a doll with that red, curly hair. I can see she looks like you," Winnie stated with a confident nod and grin.

Of course they looked alike. Annabelle and her sister both shared the same skin tone, red hair, green eyes.

Winnie's gaze darted between Annabelle and Colt before she took a step toward him. "I thought about going to see your father, unless I'm needed here."

Annabelle took a seat at the table. The bench seating made for nice family-style dining, but she had a feeling Colt didn't host too many family gatherings. She didn't know the story behind his father, and he hadn't offered to give her details, so she tried not to pay attention to the conversation behind her.

She stabbed a potato with her fork and took a bite. In

such a short time, she'd gotten used to doing things with one hand while holding Lucy or Emily with the other.

"We're good here," Colt replied. "Maybe, uh, why don't you take Dad some pie. Apple was his favorite. I don't know…"

This was the first time Annabelle had ever heard Colt even remotely sound unsure. And there was that sadness again. Colt may be a big, powerful rancher, but there was no masking the pain he obviously felt now.

"I'll take some," Winnie stated. "Let me just get that and I'll be out of your way."

Annabelle took a drink of her sweet tea and patted Lucy's back. She hated being caught in the midst of what was obviously a family moment. If anyone understood not wanting outsiders involved in a private affair, it was her.

"It was lovely to meet you."

Annabelle turned slightly, waving to Winnie. "You, too. And thanks for this wonderful meal."

"I hope you'll come back."

Before Annabelle could even reply, Winnie walked away with her container. Colt scooped hearty portions onto his plate and Annabelle stared at him, wondering what to say.

"Don't ask."

His firm command had her straightening in her seat. "I wasn't. I honestly don't know what to say. I don't know why I'm here."

Crossing the room, he set his plate down right next to hers and settled down onto the bench. "You're here because I'm tired of eating alone and I enjoy your company. You're here so you can see that you can trust me. And you're here so I can feed you."

When Annabelle reached for her fork, Colt covered her hand. Her eyes met his and he took the fork from her. When he scooped up a bite and held it in front of her lips, she froze.

"What are you doing?"

His mouth twisted into a half grin and Annabelle's heart kicked into a higher gear. "Making sure you're taken care of."

Annabelle took the bite he offered. Whatever Winnie had done to those potatoes was amazing, but it was difficult for Annabelle to concentrate with Colt sitting this close. His thigh rubbed against hers on the bench and it was all she could do not to touch it.

He fed her several more times, never taking his eyes off her as she closed her lips over the fork. Finally, she couldn't take it anymore.

"I can finish," she told him. "I'm used to holding her and eating at the same time."

"I'm getting to you."

"Yes." Why deny the truth? "Which is why I can't keep doing this."

Silence settled around them, save for the occasional clatter of their utensils against the plates. Annabelle only ate a little before she eased her legs around and came to her feet. She grabbed her plate and took it to the counter. She held on to Lucy and closed her eyes, willing some semblance of self-control to come back.

Coming here was a bad idea. She honestly didn't know what she wanted. Well, she knew, but she couldn't even go there. She had too much to worry about with her home, her father, learning about how to care for two babies. No wonder she was thinking of throwing every bit of common sense aside and letting Colt seduce her. She knew full well she'd enjoy it, that was never in question. The issue was what happened afterward? How would she work for him and try to keep the various aspects of their relationship compartmentalized?

Lucy started fussing and wiggling around. Rocking back and forth, Annabelle patted her back.

"You're really good with her."

Annabelle glanced up to see Colt standing on the other side of the island. "It's a learning process."

Wasn't that an understatement?

"What happened with the father?"

Colt's question took her completely off guard. Annabelle froze. "He's not in the picture."

"You said that, but I assume since you were engaged and now you're left alone with two babies, he wasn't man enough for the job."

Considering the father of this child and her fiancé were two different people, this could get tricky. But, she also wasn't about to get into the ordeal. She didn't intend to get too personal with Colt, and she didn't want him to look at her with pity, so there was no need to let him in on the truth behind the twins.

"The girls' father signed over all rights." That much was true. Trish had gone to him when she'd discovered she was pregnant, but he wasn't ready to be a daddy. "We're fine, though."

Because Annabelle wouldn't let them be anything but fine.

"I can't imagine any man not wanting to be with his children," Colt added, crossing his arms over his broad chest as he stared down at Lucy. "And if he was engaged to you, why would he just throw all of that away?"

"Stop," she murmured. "This isn't… I can't get into this."

Colt eased around the island and came to stand directly in front her. His eyes locked on to hers. "I'm trying to gain your trust, Annabelle. I want you to trust me when I take you to my bed."

"You're not taking me to bed," she insisted, though nerves in her stomach danced wildly at the thought.

"I am," he countered. "But I want to make sure it's my face you see, my name you say when you're there."

"Considering I've never said anyone else's name, that won't be a problem."

She hadn't meant to just blurt that out, but seeing the shock on his face was worth it.

"What?" he asked, shock lacing that single word.

She'd come this far. Might as well let him know what he was dealing with. Maybe he'd back off and get that ridiculous idea out of his head.

"I'm a virgin."

Eleven

Very little in Colt's life shocked him. He'd traveled all over the globe, dealt with a variety of people and liked to believe he could think on his feet. But nothing prepared him for the confusing statement Annabelle had just dropped between them.

"How the hell is that even possible?" he asked. "I know the girls aren't adopted. They look just like you."

Annabelle patted the sleeping baby and nodded. "No, they're not adopted. My sister was their mother."

Her sister. The one who passed away.

Colt attempted to make things clear in his head, but he was at a loss. How the hell did he respond to that? She was clearly out of her depth with so much, having life throw things at her she wasn't ready for—motherhood…sex.

And he was an ass for being so forward, so blatant.

Well, he was a jerk for other things as well, but that was business.

In his defense, how the hell was he supposed to know she was so inexperienced? She had babies, for crying out loud, and the way she'd flirted, kissed...

"I don't know what to say."

Annabelle held his gaze as she rested her cheek against the sleeping baby's head. "There's nothing to say. You needed to know what you were up against. Clearly, I'm not swayed by easy charms and sexy men. So, you'd probably be better off moving on to a woman who will actually give in to your advances."

Colt would've laughed had her statement held any conviction or had she not melted against him when they'd kissed. Annabelle was already giving in to his every advance, whether she wanted to admit it or not.

"You think because you're inexperienced that I'll move on?" he asked, taking a step closer until his chest brushed the arm she held Lucy with. "Baby, if anything, I want you more. To know I can be the one to show you everything, I've never been more turned on."

"Don't call me *baby*," she whispered.

"When I get you into my bed, I'll call you your name and you'll damn well love every second of it."

She jerked back. "You're not seriously still interested in me. You just want the challenge."

"It's true I've never backed away from a challenge," he assured her. "But I want you, sweetness. I've wanted you from the moment you plowed into my fence. And you want me, too, or you wouldn't have stared at my bare chest so long that day."

Her eyes narrowed. "If I weren't holding Lucy, I'd smack you."

Colt believed she probably would. He couldn't help but laugh as he leaned close to her ear. "Save that energy."

"You're impossible." Annabelle took a step back, then shifted Lucy in her arms. "I'm going home. Tell Winnie thanks for dinner and I'll get her that recipe."

"Why didn't you tell me you like to cook?" he asked, the thought of her leaving suddenly unbearable.

"I never said I liked to cook," she retorted.

He leaned against the edge of the counter, feigning calm and giving her a bit more breathing room.

"You didn't have to," he stated. "You baked bread and brought it back. Someone who hates cooking wouldn't have done that."

Annabelle bit her bottom lip as if she were contemplating letting him into her personal life any further. She'd already dropped a bomb. What did it matter at this point?

"I actually love to bake," she told him. "Bread is my weakness. My mother always baked bread. Our house always smelled amazing. I guess I just want to keep up that tradition, and hopefully pass it down to the girls one day."

The importance of family traditions. That was definitely something he understood, something his father had instilled into each of his children.

"The girls are lucky to have you," Colt told her. "I'm sorry about your sister."

He'd already apologized, but knowing more about the situation gave him another tug on his conscience. Damn it.

"I don't want to talk about her."

There was something in Annabelle's tone that had him cocking his head and studying her. The sadness was there, but something else, too, something almost bitter or resentful.

"Do you want to lay her on the sofa?" he suggested. "We can talk while she rests."

"You just want to talk? Don't you think we've exhausted all the topics for the night? Unless you'd like to ask about my father's gambling. Better yet, why don't we talk about your father or why you have a limp."

The limp he could discuss, but he didn't want to talk about his father. He missed the man his father once was, and discussing him, given his current mental state, wasn't Colt's idea of a good time.

"Your father is a gambler and mine has dementia. That sums up that topic." He pulled in a deep breath. "As for the limp, when a tornado ripped through Stone River last year, our main barn was torn up. I was helping to rebuild it when I fell off a ladder, shattering my hip bone and breaking my back. I'm still getting back to normal…if that's even possible."

Before she could offer pity, which he did not want, Colt opted to throw the focus back on her. He glanced down toward her half-empty plate. "You didn't eat enough."

Annabelle shrugged. "I haven't had much of an appetite lately."

"Which is why you passed out."

"You're not going to let that go, are you?"

Colt shook his head. "Not until I see you're taking care of yourself properly."

Annabelle wrapped both arms around Lucy as she turned and headed toward the patio off the kitchen. Colt followed, pleased she'd given up on the idea of just flat out leaving. For reasons he didn't want to examine too closely, he wanted her there, in his home. Annabelle took a seat on the sofa and laid Lucy down beside her. After making a wall with throw pillows, Annabelle settled against the cushion and tipped her head back.

"It feels so good to sit and do nothing."

Colt remained in the doorway, leaning against the frame. She looked so peaceful. Surprisingly, having Annabelle and Lucy there didn't feel awkward. The women he dated didn't have children, but Lucy was so damn adorable, it was impossible not to be lighter, happier in her presence. Both girls were precious and obviously so loved by Annabelle. She'd clearly do anything to keep them from harm.

But as Colt studied Annabelle, something shifted inside him. She was making him feel, she was making him want and that wasn't going to work. He didn't want to start thinking of her beyond business or the bedroom.

Maybe having her there wasn't the best idea. He still wanted her, that wouldn't go away until he'd gotten her out of his system. But he'd learned more about her, quite a bit, and she made him want to take care of her.

She made it nearly impossible not to admire her acts of selflessness.

Annabelle Carter was one of the most amazing people he'd ever met.

And she'd just let out a most unladylike snore.

Colt stepped down onto the enclosed patio and stood over her. Her mouth was softer when she slept, her light lashes fanned out over her cheeks, her chest rose and fell so lightly, so steadily. She'd worn herself completely out.

Lucy whimpered and Colt's gaze jerked to the baby who was starting to wake up. Fear gripped him. He didn't want to wake Annabelle and he didn't want Lucy to start crying.

When Lucy started squirming even more, her eyes opened and she whimpered once again.

Colt instantly lifted her from the sofa. Throw pillows slid to the floor as he hurried from the room. Annabelle needed sleep, probably more than she needed to eat. But what the hell did he know about babies? Fussy babies at that.

As he headed through the kitchen and to the front of the house toward the diaper bag, Colt figured he was about to find out.

Annabelle woke with a start. She glanced around the large room surrounded by windows and filled with indoor plants. Then she recalled she was at Colt's house.

Her focus shifted to the sofa cushion beside her where Lucy had been. The pillow barrier had fallen to the floor.

Pushing her hair away from her face, Annabelle came to her feet and smoothed her shirt back into place. She had no clue how long she'd been out. The last thing she remembered was sitting down for a second and Colt leaning against the door frame. She'd wanted just a moment to relax before heading home.

After dropping the bomb about her personal life, she figured he'd be done with her, but apparently not. He said he wanted company, that he enjoyed talking with her. And she had to admit, as much as she hated owing him money, she enjoyed their talks, as well. Who was she kidding? She enjoyed more than their talks. She enjoyed the way her body tingled when he entered the room. Enjoyed the way his slightest touch fired up her every nerve ending. She only wished they'd gotten to know each other under different circumstances.

But this was the hand she was dealt. Unfortunately, she had no idea what card to lay down next.

Annabelle stepped up into the kitchen. Colt wasn't around. She headed through the wide hallway, not having a clue where he'd be. She wasn't worried, she knew Colt had a handle on Lucy or he would've woken her up. At least, she hoped that's what he would've done.

A wave of embarrassment swept over her. She'd obviously been even more exhausted than she'd first thought.

Glancing at a large wall clock at the end of the hallway, Annabelle realized she'd probably been asleep nearly an hour. She knew it had gotten later because the sun was setting, based on the pink and orange glow streaming in through the windows.

"Colt," she called out. She heard absolutely nothing as she peeked in various doors and headed down another hall.

When Annabelle stepped into the spacious living room, she stood in awe of an entire wall of bookshelves. The amount of cookbooks she could fill those with made her baker's heart speed up.

But she'd never be filling those shelves with anything. Pebblebrook wasn't her house. She'd do well to cling to the home she had.

As her eyes swept over the room, she stilled when her gaze landed on the set of patio doors leading out to the side yard. With the sun setting, the magical glow stretching across the horizon and cattle like little black dots in the distance, Annabelle's breath caught in her throat.

Colt stood beneath an old oak tree. He was cradling Lucy in one strong arm and feeding her a bottle. Annabelle had never witnessed a sexier sight than this man holding the child that had become her own.

Tears pricked her eyes as she gripped the handle of the patio door. She wanted to take in this moment, pretend that it wasn't fleeting. What would it be like if this were her home? If Colt wanted her for more than sex, more than her land?

He'd be an amazing father. Obviously he'd taken Lucy so Annabelle could sleep. How could that act of kindness not make her look at him a different way? How could she not find herself even more attracted to him?

But she was realistic. In just a few months, she'd have her debt paid off and he'd have no use for her. If she slept with him, well, she didn't know what would happen because she'd never been in that situation before. She obviously wasn't a casual-sex person, but nearly every part of her wanted to know what being with Colt would be like. She had a pretty good imagination.

Pulling in a deep breath and praying for strength where that man was concerned, Annabelle opened the patio door and stepped outside. When she started making her way across the yard, Colt turned and met her gaze. His smile nearly had her knees buckling. That man could do so much without ever laying a hand on her.

"I'm sorry I fell asleep on you," she told him as she drew closer.

"I won't take it personally." He glanced back down at Lucy who patted the side of her bottle with her chubby hand. "It got a little hairy when I was trying to hold her and read the directions on the formula can. I'm thankful you already had water in the bottle, so I hope I did everything right."

Annabelle stepped closer, catching Lucy's eyes. The instant their eyes locked, the infant smiled, milk streaming down the side of her mouth.

"Oops." Annabelle laughed as she reached for the baby and the bottle. "She tends to get sidetracked easily."

Colt swiped the dribble of milk from his forearm and shrugged. "I work with farm animals. I'm not afraid of a little formula on my arm."

Annabelle took over feeding Lucy. She loved looking down into those green eyes. Loved seeing her sister's reflection. For the past twenty-four years, Trish had been Annabelle's best friend. At some point, she'd have to forgive her sister for her betrayal, but she wasn't quite there yet. It was too fresh, too soon.

But raising her babies was easing the pain, it was bridging that gap even though her sister wasn't there. Annabelle knew in time, she'd forgive Trish, because there was no way to care for those babies and still hold ill feelings.

"My sister and my fiancé were killed in a car accident."

She didn't know why she just blurted that out. Maybe she thought it would be therapeutic to get her feelings out in the open.

"They were seeing each other behind my back." Okay, that didn't make her feel any better at all. If anything, now she felt like a fool. "I didn't know they were involved until the day of the accident. We got into an argument. My sister was crying, Matt was trying to justify their actions. Then they left and that was the last time I saw either of them."

Colt took a step toward her, but Annabelle kept her gaze on sweet Lucy. She didn't want to look up and see pity in Colt's eyes.

"Annabelle…"

She smiled. "Now you use my name?"

"I'm sorry," he said, not a trace of humor in his voice. "I had no idea about this. I just knew your sister had passed away."

"It's crazy. For so long, I looked up to her, wanted to be like her. She was a wonderful mother to Emily and Lucy. I couldn't wait to get married and start my own family."

She'd have to wait a little longer for that. She had plenty of other things to get straightened out in her life first.

"After the wedding, I planned to come back here and get my business off the ground."

"What business?"

Annabelle shook her head, meeting Colt's worried gaze. "It's nothing."

He reached out, curling his hand around her shoulder. "It's something important enough to bring you back home."

It was everything. The dream her mother had had, the affection she'd had in her voice when she'd talk about opening the B and B, the people that would hopefully fill it and enjoy the beauty that Stone River had to offer.

"Tell me."

The command was delivered so softly, she knew he cared or he wouldn't pursue the issue.

"A bed-and-breakfast," she murmured, looking back down at Lucy. With the bottle nearly empty, Annabelle pulled it from Lucy's puckered lips and eased the baby upright. "It was a goal my mother had before she passed. She taught me how to bake, telling me that's what would be the heart of our business. People who came to stay with us would want good food. I couldn't wait to grow up and help her run the place. After she passed, I was nervous to do it all alone. But this past year, I got engaged and thought it was time to just go for it."

Holding Lucy on her hip, Annabelle looked out to

the horizon and forced her emotions down. She didn't want to break here, not in front of Colt.

"Over the past few months, these setbacks nearly destroyed me. But I know my mom wouldn't want me to give up, so I'm not. I'm doing all of this for her."

That last word came out broken as tears clogged her throat. Apparently she wasn't as strong as she thought.

"I don't know what to say," he murmured, squeezing her shoulder.

Annabelle turned her attention back to him. "There's nothing to say. Life sometimes has other plans for us. If I gave up each time I had a stumbling block, I would've thrown in the towel a long time ago."

Colt's bright blue eyes studied her and Annabelle wanted to know what was going through his mind. Did he see her as weak because she couldn't hold on to the life she'd wanted? Did he think she was pathetic because she had no real vision at the moment? Her life was in chaos and there was no clear picture in sight.

"You're one of the most remarkable people I've ever known," he stated.

Lucy tugged on Annabelle's hair and pulled some into her mouth. Annabelle eased the strands from the baby's clutches and pushed them behind her shoulders.

"Then you don't know too many people," she laughed.

Colt's hand trailed up to cup the side of her face. "I know people all over the world. None of them has half the tenacity for life that you do."

Such a compliment coming from Colt Elliott warmed her…as if she needed to be warmed in any more areas where he was concerned.

He leaned in, and Annabelle knew he was going to kiss her. She shifted Lucy slightly on her hip and tipped her head to meet Colt's lips. The gentle way he swept his mouth across hers while stroking his thumb along her jawline…yeah, that man was powerful without being forceful. He made her want things. Things that she would never have with him.

When he eased back, Annabelle knew she needed to go. If she stayed any longer, she'd start getting delusions that this life could be hers, that she could live on a sprawling ranch like Pebblebrook. That a man like Colt could fall in love with her. This wasn't a fairy tale. This was real life and she was crawling day after day to get hers back.

"I need to go," she stated, licking her lips to taste him once more. "Thanks for dinner."

He dropped his hand and stepped back. "I'm sure Winnie would love for you to come back again."

"And you?" She couldn't resist asking. "Would you love for me to come back again?"

Heat filled his eyes as he stared at her mouth. "I think you already know the answer to that."

Yeah, she did. And Annabelle knew if she came back for dinner, she would not be bringing a baby.

Twelve

Annabelle rifled through her purse before work the next morning. She needed a pen to jot down that recipe for Winnie, but she couldn't find one.

She also couldn't find the fifty dollar bill she'd had in there yesterday. She'd given her father some money for the store, and he'd put the change back like she'd told him to. She hated immediately thinking he took the cash, but she knew full well she didn't use it. Where had she been besides the barn, Colt's house and her house?

Dread filled her stomach.

Annabelle sank on the edge of her bed. She was going to have to confront him. She'd not only looked in her purse that had been on her bed, she'd looked all around the bed, beneath the bed, thinking maybe it had fallen out.

She should've known better than to leave cash around, but she'd sincerely hoped he was trying to be a better man, be the father she'd asked him to be.

Annabelle didn't know if she wanted to cry or throw her hands in the air and give up.

She grabbed her phone from the nightstand and texted Colt to tell him there had been an emergency and she'd drive herself over a little bit later. Shoving her phone in the pocket of her jeans, she cast a glance at Emily and Lucy, still sleeping in their cribs against the far wall. Both girls tended to wake once a night to eat and since they'd both gotten up at four and were wide-awake until six, they now opted to sleep in. Of course they fell asleep right when she needed to get ready to go to the farm.

The scent of coffee filtered up from the first floor—a sure sign her father was awake. She took a few minutes to compose herself before she went into full attack mode.

Pulling in a breath, Annabelle went downstairs and into the kitchen. Her father had his back to her as he poured himself a mug of coffee.

"Did you take money from my purse?"

His shoulders stiffened. "You gave me money for the store. I put the change back like you said."

The fact that he evaded her question told her everything she needed to know. Her heart sank—and her hopes weren't far behind.

"What was it this time, Dad? A ball game? A horse race? Online poker?"

Neil Carter dropped his head between his shoulders. "I'll pay you back. I know that investment will return—"

"It's not an investment, Dad," she all but yelled. "We have no extra money. I'm not only paying off this house, I'm trying to raise two babies now. When will you be a responsible adult? When will you see that this habit of yours is destroying us? Because it doesn't matter how much I want you to change, you have to want it, too."

Could he not see that this wasn't just about him or her anymore? Emily and Lucy needed them—they had no other family. No matter what happened with the farm, with the gambling, Annabelle vowed to hold strong. She would not fail those babies. She loved them like they were her own, and she wanted to honor her sister's memory, despite what had gone down in those final days.

Her father set the mug on the counter and turned to face her. "I do, Belle. It's just going to take time."

The subtle tap on her front door had Annabelle cringing. Colt. No doubt he'd shown up even though she told him she'd be late.

"Time is something we don't have," she whispered before turning away.

"Belle," he called after her.

"I have to go to work," she stated without looking back as she headed to the front door. "Someone has to hold this family together."

Considering she only had a few ones in her purse, she wasn't even bothering to take it. He could have her last dollar. What did it matter at this point? The money for the house wasn't even going through her hands. Colt was keeping her wages, so at least that was something. But she didn't have any extra and she knew she'd have to go to the store soon. Not to mention the bills would be coming due. Apparently, her father had no respect for such necessities as water and electricity.

Annabelle jerked the door open, causing Colt to jump back. She stormed past him, ignoring his questioning gaze. The sooner she got to the ranch, the sooner she could work out her frustrations.

"Hold up, sweetheart."

She whirled around on Colt. "Not today. Do not start with the pet names. I'm not in the mood."

The black hat shaded half of his face, but those eyes still managed to pierce her. "Care to tell me why you look like you want to kill someone?"

Annabelle closed her eyes and blew out a breath. "Not really. Just…get me out of here."

Colt opened his mouth to say something, but finally nodded. Annabelle turned and mounted Lightning before Colt got on behind her.

The instant his arms came around to grab the reins, Annabelle leaned back against his chest. She didn't care if this made her weak.

"Not a word," she muttered. "I just need this for a second."

"Lean on me all you want."

With a flick of his wrists, he set Lightning into a soft trot. Annabelle fought back tears. If her father didn't get his act together, she didn't know what they'd do. She couldn't pay off this house and keep them afloat if he was pilfering money. Annabelle had already hidden her mother's emerald ring. If her father found that, she hated to admit that he'd probably hock it.

"I was going to drive in a few minutes late," she told him after a bit.

"When you said emergency, I was afraid something was wrong with one of the girls. You didn't specify, so I went ahead and came anyway."

"I'm a mess, Colt. I'm more of a hindrance than help at this point."

He grasped the reins in one hand and wrapped his free arm around her waist, hugging her into his body. "Why this negativity? That's not like you."

"Just a morning dose of reality. And I haven't even had my coffee, yet."

She started to ease up when his arm tightened. "You're fine right here, darlin'."

"What did I tell you about the names?" she asked, the fight gone from her voice as she settled back against him.

"I think my nicknames are growing on you."

She couldn't help but smile. "Don't get too cocky."

They rode another moment in silence and her heart sank when they approached the barn. She could've kept riding, pretended nothing was going on in the world. For just a little bit she wanted to imagine her problems, her father's problems, weren't gnawing at her heels as she tried to outrun them.

"Something happen with your father?" Colt asked softly.

Annabelle sat up, mostly because if Josh or Ryan were in the barns, she didn't want them to see her nes-

tled against their boss. Although she figured they knew
something was up. It wasn't normal for a man to pick
up a woman on horseback for work.

Funny how she'd not only gotten used to it, she actually looked forward to their rides.

"I'd rather not get into it," she stated as she focused
on the stone building ahead. "What do you have planned
today?"

"Something you've never done before," he promised.
"You up for a ride on Genesis?"

"Sure. Anytime I get to ride is great."

Colt brought Lightning to a stop and dismounted before reaching a hand out to assist Annabelle. She let the
touch linger. She'd take all the Colt she could get today.

"I left without grabbing a hat."

Colt patted Lightning as he looped his reins around
the post outside the barn. "You won't need one today."

Confused, Annabelle blinked and crossed her arms
over her tank. "I won't?"

"Nope. Go get Genesis ready. I'll meet you back
here. I need to give some final orders to Ryan and Josh
before we take off."

The man was intriguing, and she had a feeling that's
exactly how he wanted to be seen. He wanted to keep
her on her toes. Another reason she needed to be ready
at all times for whatever he threw her way.

Colt didn't recall being nervous about anything in
his life. He'd been angry and frustrated when Layla
had left, he'd been hurt when his father slipped into a
tragic state of mind and he'd been worried each time

his brother Hayes was deployed. Even when his twin brother, Beau, had a movie opening in LA, Colt didn't have a bundle of nerves dancing in his stomach.

But today he was a mess. He was going to take Annabelle to a portion of the property that was rarely seen unless you specifically ventured back there. It was behind Hayes's house, stretching along the riverbank that ran on the edge of their property.

It was the most peaceful spot on the ranch. After Annabelle opened up emotionally at their dinner last night, he wanted to just relax with her. Forget the fact they were boss and employee. He wanted her to trust him.

Stupid of him really, considering his intentions hadn't changed one bit. But there was a part of him that wanted her to talk to him, to tell him her fears, her needs…her desires.

When he'd been in the yard feeding Lucy, Colt had been smacked in the face with a dose of reality. He did want a family, that wasn't news to him, but he wanted it sooner rather than later. Maybe his life didn't have to be in perfect order before he found someone to settle down with.

And he certainly wasn't saying he wanted Annabelle and the twins as his family. That would never work even if he'd had those thoughts. But holding Lucy just had him thinking and wondering if he could have it all and throw out the timeline he'd given himself.

Pushing his thoughts aside, he pulled out his phone and shot off a group text to Josh and Ryan. The edging around the landscaping needed trimming and the vet was due this afternoon to check on the steers once again. A fairly simple day, but Colt knew that not every day on the ranch could be predictable. Even if you had plans, sometimes livestock and Mother Nature had other ideas.

Just as he shoved his phone back into his pocket, Annabelle stepped out of the barn. Leading Genesis, she focused that bright green gaze on him. The punch of lust each time she looked at him never lessened. And to know she was untouched only made him ache for her even more.

How had someone so sexy, so damn passionate, gone all this time without giving herself to a man? More important, what type of man had been with her and not been able to pull out that desire? She practically dissolved in a puddle at his feet when he touched her, and he wasn't too proud to admit the feeling was mutual. She did something to him, something that made him want to possess her in a primal way.

"Where to, boss?"

He loved when she called him that. As if she surrendered to his power and fully accepted that he was in charge.

"Mount up and follow me."

He hated that he wouldn't reap the benefits of riding behind her, but she had no idea this little place even existed and he had to be the one to lead the way.

Colt pushed himself back up onto Lightning and set off to the east side of the land.

He called over his shoulder, "It will take us some time to get there, but I promise it will be worth the wait."

"No problem. I'm enjoying the view."

Colt sent her a wink. If she was going to flirt so blatantly, he sure as hell was going to return the gesture. He figured she was doing anything to forget what happened this morning with her father. Whatever had gone on, it must have been something major for her to be so angry when he'd picked her up. She seemed to want to stay mum about it so Colt would have to draw his own conclusions.

He just hoped like hell Neil Carter wasn't gambling again. Not now. Now when Annabelle was literally busting her ass to save his.

After about fifteen minutes, they reached Hayes's house. It would be good to have his brother home for good. Colt only prayed he managed to adjust to being back and settling into civilian life.

"This is the house your father grew up in?" Annabelle asked.

"My grandfather had it built when he started ranching." Colt pointed to the old oak tree to the side of the house. "That tire swing has seen many years and every Elliott kid. It's just a neat location the way it's tucked between the river and the brook."

This house could tell stories. Colt figured one day Hayes would tear it down to rebuild, and Colt couldn't blame him, but he hoped he'd keep it and just put his home on another section of the ranch.

"I love this house."

Annabelle's wistful tone had him smiling. She appreciated the finer things, and he didn't mean expensive. She saw the beauty in everything. His ex, on the other hand, had had a taste for pricey, designer clothing, flashy cars, trips all over. He didn't mind pampering the woman in his life, but he expected he'd be her top priority...not his bank account.

"We can stop here." Colt made sure the horses were in the shade beneath one of the large oaks before looping the reins around the hooks. "We'll walk to the place I want to show you."

When he looked back, Annabelle was staring down at him, her head tilted in question. Colt crossed the distance between them and extended his hand.

"Trust me."

The two words were so simple, yet so complex, considering their relationship. She shouldn't trust him. She should hate him with every ounce of her being. He wished things were different, he wished she'd never come back into the picture because taking things from Neil didn't bother Colt's conscience one bit. But knowing he was going to take the land that was the foundation for Annabelle's dream...that twisted something inside of him that he didn't want to face.

Part of him couldn't help but wonder what his father would think. His dad had been determined to make this dude ranch a reality, but he was also a family man first.

Damn it. Colt couldn't think like that. He and Annabelle couldn't be more even if that's what he wanted. Once she discovered the truth, she'd hate him.

Annabelle slid her leg over the side of the horse and Colt gripped her waist to help her down. He stepped closer behind her, aligning their bodies perfectly.

"Is this why you brought me out here alone?" she

asked, turning her face just enough for him see her half-grin.

"I've never brought a woman to my brother's house for sex." That much was completely true. "What I have to show you is in the back."

Without asking, he took her hand in his and led her around the side of the house.

"Oh, my word," she gasped. "It's beautiful."

The river curved around the property as if framing it with crystal clear water. An old stone outbuilding sat right on the riverbank at the edge of the property. The original stone wall ran along the edge of the property line.

"It's peaceful. I figured you could use some of that in your life."

Annabelle turned to face him fully, still holding on to his hand. "How do you know when I need anything? Dinner, a nap, a quiet place to relax. I'm going to get fired for not working if you keep this up."

He'd never fire her. And he wasn't sure he wanted to let her go at the end of this three-month period, either. She was a hard worker. Granted, she had her home as motivation, but he was going to hate to lose her.

And not just for the business. Cutting her out of his life would hurt and he'd have to learn to cope with the mess he'd made.

As Annabelle glanced back out onto the water, a strand of hair blew across her bottom lip, and before Colt could think better of it, he swiped it away. His fingertip grazed her mouth, sending a jolt of desire through him.

Her eyes swept back around and met his. "You did bring me out here to seduce me," she murmured.

Colt slipped his hand along her jawline, threading his fingers through her hair. "I didn't. But you've been seducing me since the moment you ran into my fence."

"I don't know what to do."

That whispered admission was the green light he'd been waiting for, the one he hadn't seen coming. But he sure as hell wasn't going to give her time to change her mind.

"Listen to your body," he told her, stepping into her. "What's your body telling you right now?"

A small smile spread across her lips. "That I want your shirt off again."

Colt laughed. "I can deal with that."

He tugged the shirt from his jeans and unbuttoned it, keeping his eyes on hers the entire time. Once he dropped it to the ground, he propped his hands on his hips. The approving once-over she gave him had him ready to rip off the black tank she wore. It was only fair.

"I've never known a man to look so hot in just a hat, jeans, and boots."

He didn't know what to say to that, so he slid his fingertips up her bare arms. "How slow do we need to take this?" he asked. "Because I don't want you scared and you deserve to get full enjoyment."

She shivered beneath his touch. "I'm enjoying this pretty well right now."

Oh, she was going to be so damn fun. His body trembled with need. He wanted this woman more than anyone he'd ever been with. He didn't know if it was the thrill of being her first or just the fact that this was Annabelle. Probably both. But he wasn't going to waste time in his head analyzing his every thought.

He had a woman to strip.

"Just…tell me if I do something wrong. Okay?"

Colt stilled. There was a hesitation to her voice that he didn't like.

"Are you sure about this?" he asked. "Because I don't want you to feel pressured. You have to want this as much as I do or we're done."

She reached down, tugged on the hem of her tank, and flung the garment over her head. Standing before him in a plain white bra and jeans with her hair around her shoulders, Colt had never seen a sexier sight.

"I'm nervous, but I know what I want," she told him. "So do what you want to me and I'll tell you if it's too much. Deal?"

Do what he wanted? Oh, hell yes, that was a deal.

Unable to wait another second, Colt slid his hands around the dip in her waist and tugged her until she was flush against his chest. Finally. Skin to skin. She was all curves and all his.

Colt captured her mouth and willed himself to slow down. He had an ache for this woman and he couldn't go into this like she'd been his every fantasy for days. He had to take his time, to make sure she got as much pleasure as he could possibly give.

Thirteen

Annabelle had never been so nervous and anxious at the same time. Colt's mouth magically moved over hers. There was an urgency in his kiss, yet she could tell he was restraining himself.

She eased her mouth from his and framed his face. "I'm not fragile. Don't hold back."

His eyes held hers for the briefest of moments before he picked her up. She couldn't help the squeal that escaped her. Instinct had her looping her hands behind his neck and wondering if he was shooting for romance.

This wasn't romance, though. This was nothing more than her finally giving in to a need she'd had for some time and it had never been stronger than with Colt Elliott.

For once, she was going to take exactly what she wanted, when she wanted it. Consequences be damned.

Colt carried her behind the house, his gait a bit off.

"Put me down," she told him.

"In a minute."

"You're limping."

He stopped, holding her so securely against him, and turned his focus to her eyes, her lips. "Sweetness, let me do this right."

Part of her wondered how many times he called other lovers by these names. He'd claimed none, but Colt was a natural charmer. Still, there was something that blossomed inside her at the idea that he only used those terms for her.

Annabelle closed her eyes and rested her head against his shoulder. What was she thinking? This wasn't the pivotal moment that would lead to a happily-ever-after for them.

Colt made her feel sexy and he wanted her. It was all that simple and that wonderful.

He started off again until he came to the riverbank. When he set her down, he nipped at her lips as if he couldn't get enough. Her chest rubbed against his and she couldn't help but arch against him.

"Wait right here," he muttered against her mouth.

He darted back around the house and Annabelle felt rather foolish standing there with her jeans, boots and bra. She waited a minute, wondering where he went, when he finally came back carrying the blanket that had been beneath her horse's saddle.

She couldn't help but laugh. "I figure you didn't plan this or you would've had something already set up."

"I really didn't plan this," he laughed. With a swift

jerk, he fanned the blanket out over the ground. "But I'm damn sure not going to let this moment go."

When he turned back and raked his eyes over her, Annabelle had never felt such a jolt in her life. He may as well have touched her with his hands, his mouth. Anticipation curled deep in her stomach.

"Maybe you could help me undress, that would help." She went for the snap on her jeans. "Or maybe we should just—"

"No." Colt closed the space between them and eased her hands aside. "This belongs to me."

"Me, or getting me naked?"

He jerked the snap open, keeping his gaze on hers. "Everything."

Just as she processed his words, he reached behind her and flicked her bra open. Nerves fell away. Colt's intense stare, his passion and need, they all combined to make her forget she should be nervous. Ache replaced her anxiety and she wanted more.

Annabelle toed her boots off and watched as Colt reached for his belt buckle.

"Wait," she told him. "Shouldn't I get to return the favor?"

He shook his head with a laugh. "Honey, if you touch me right now, this will go faster than either of us wants."

"Maybe I'm ready for fast."

Where had that breathy voice come from? Was she seriously that girl? That flirty vixen? Apparently, with Colt she was another person, but this felt so right.

He slid his thumbs inside the waistband of her jeans. As his rough fingertips grazed her skin, Annabelle trembled. Colt jerked her pants down, pulling her panties with them.

When he dropped to his knees and removed the rest of her clothes, Annabelle pulled in a breath and willed herself to remain calm. She certainly didn't want to make a complete fool of herself right now. Between the ache and the nerves, she wasn't sure what to do, what to say.

But when she stood before him naked and Colt remained on his knees, sampling her with his heavy-lidded gaze, Annabelle knew for a fact that she held the control. He was giving her the reins, so to speak.

She dropped to her knees in front of him and curled her hands around his shoulders. "Touch me," she whispered.

Colt cursed his shaky hands. He finally had Annabelle naked before him and he was nervous. He'd never been nervous with a woman before, not even when he was a virgin. He'd always been about pleasuring his partner, being in control.

But with Annabelle, something was different. Something he didn't want to think about. He only wanted Annabelle, right here, right now.

Colt captured her mouth beneath his as he lowered her back to the blanket. Extending his arms to the ground, he caught himself before he could fully put his weight on her. Wrapping her slender arms around his neck, she threaded her fingers through his hair.

Colt pulled back, glancing down at the beauty laid

out before him. He came back to his feet and quickly shed the rest of his clothes and boots. Annabelle's eyes roamed over his bare body. That passion he saw in her eyes only amped up his ache for her.

Despite the fact she told him to do anything, Colt had to have some semblance of self-control. He'd never taken an inexperienced woman before.

With her hair fanned out all around her, Annabelle reached for him. Colt grabbed his pants, pulled a condom from his wallet and covered himself. He dropped between her knees, took her hands in his, and stretched her arms above her head. She arched at the adjustment and it was all Colt could do not to devour her.

"You're driving me crazy," she stated through gritted teeth.

"At least I'm not alone," he muttered.

He used his knees to shove her legs wider. His free hand trailed up her inner thigh, instantly causing her to tremble beneath his touch. When he found her center, Annabelle's eyes drifted shut as she let out a moan.

Yes. That's exactly the response he wanted. Her hips tilted, urging him for more. He leaned down, placing his mouth on her stomach and trailing his lips up to her breasts. Her hands jerked beneath his grip as if she wanted loose from her restraints.

"Not so fast," he murmured against her heated skin. "I'm not done and you can't touch me just yet."

"I need…"

"I need," he agreed. "Too much."

So much, that he wasn't about to reveal everything

on his mind. Hell, he wasn't even sure what he was thinking because he was trying *not* to think it.

When Colt removed his hand from between her legs, she let out a whimper. She was so ready and he…damn if he wasn't eager to show her what she'd been missing. He wanted to freeze that moment. To lock away this second of her staring up at him with such desire. He'd never felt so wanted before. Definitely not with…

No. He wasn't bringing any other woman into the picture, not even in his mind. Annabelle was perfection. She was his.

Everything else in the outside world didn't exist for him. Not the farm, not the potential dude ranch, not his brothers or even his father. There was nothing, no one but Annabelle.

Releasing her wrists, he placed both of his hands on either side of her face as he settled between her thighs.

"Tell me you're okay with this." Because if she wasn't completely on board, he'd stop. It would kill him, but she called the shots here. "You want me to keep going?"

"Don't even think of leaving me like this," she panted. "Finish what you started."

Music to his ears. Slowly, Colt joined their bodies. He kept his eyes on hers, waiting for a sign that she needed him to stop.

But her eyes merely widened as she bit her lower lip. Her hips jerked up to meet his and a low, sexy groan escaped her. Colt gritted his teeth. The agony of not claiming her the way his body needed to was excruciating. He wanted to gather her up and have her wrap those long, lean legs around his waist as he made her his.

Next time, he vowed. Because there would be a next time.

Annabelle lifted her knees on either side of him as she rocked her hips. "I told you not to hold back."

"I'm hurting you."

Her eyes held his as a smile danced around her mouth. "You're torturing me. I need this. I need you. Now move."

Colt nipped at her lips. "Whatever you say, sweetness."

"Don't—"

He crushed his mouth against hers as her arms looped around his neck. Colt quickened the pace, finally. He relished the sting of her fingertips on his skin. He wanted her to feel, to make him feel. They came together perfectly and she was certainly holding her own.

"Wrap your legs around me," he demanded against her lips. "Now."

As she circled his waist, locking her ankles behind his back, Colt pumped faster. Her little pants and whimpers spurred him on as she matched his rhythm.

"Colt."

"Right here, baby."

Her taut body beneath his trembled, then tightened. She tipped her head back and closed her eyes.

"Look at me," he commanded.

When that green gaze came back to his, Colt tried not to get lost in the depths there. Tried not to see exactly what was staring back at him, because it was definitely more than just sex. There were feelings. Feelings that he sure as hell didn't want to see.

Colt leaned down to run his lips along the side of her neck, across her chest. She cried out his name as her body stilled, her nails biting deeper into his shoulders.

Thrusting again, Colt shattered right along with her. This was exactly what he wanted, what he could control. All the feelings and emotions had no place here.

As her tremors ceased, Colt gathered her close, inhaling her jasmine scent. As much as his instincts told him to flee, he wasn't that big of a jerk. This was her time—he couldn't help if everything he saw in her eyes scared the hell out of him.

He prayed she didn't have some crazy notion that this meant anything more than just sex. He couldn't let her believe they had a future. Acting on their attraction had been inevitable, but he hadn't said anything up front about not getting involved. He had plans, damn it, and they didn't include getting wrapped up in those expressive green eyes.

But there was still that part deep inside him that could want more…with her.

Colt eased to the side, pulling her in his arms. He wasn't one to cuddle, but again, he wasn't about to be a jerk. He just needed to relax and consider his next step.

And that nugget of emotion circling his conscience could shut the hell up.

Fourteen

Colt was already having regrets.

Even though he hadn't said a word, he didn't need to. Annabelle lay against his chest, feeling his heart beat beneath her cheek and Colt was miles away—mentally at least.

His entire body was rigid and she knew he didn't want to be there. Didn't want to be holding her. The pity snuggle was not working for her and she refused to ever be made a fool of by a man again.

Annabelle sat up, causing Colt's arm to fall away. She smoothed her hair back from her face and attempted to radiate confidence she didn't feel. When it came to intimacy, she had zero experience, but her body was still humming…while he was silently stewing beside her.

If he was having regrets or doubts about what had happened, that was on him. Not her problem.

Coming to her feet, Annabelle purposely didn't look back at him. Bad enough she was walking around the riverbank retrieving her clothes, she didn't want to see guilt in his eyes.

What a fool. How could she think a man like Colt Elliott would actually want to be with someone like her? He'd known exactly how to touch her, what to say, and just how forceful to be.

She'd relished every single moment.

Annabelle jerked her panties on, then wrestled back into her bra. Clutching her jeans to her chest, she whirled around to see him sitting up on the blanket watching her.

"If you're sorry this happened, just keep it to yourself."

Not a care in the world that he was as naked as the day he was born, Colt lifted a knee and propped an arm across it. "I'm not sorry this happened."

"Did I do something wrong?" she asked, heat flooding her cheeks. "Because you're not exactly giving off a vibe like you had a good time."

Like a panther, he rose and stalked toward her. "I had a good time, darlin'. I just didn't want you to get the impression that this meant more than what it was."

It took a second for his words to sink in, but when they did, rage boiled within her.

"Are you kidding me?" she asked, swatting her hand on his bare chest. "You think you show me a good time by the river on your family's property and I'm going to be head over heels in love with you? You do have quite the ego, Colt. I'm not going to start planning our wedding, so relax."

She hated to admit, even to herself, that she could see herself falling for him. She hadn't gotten there, yet, but it could happen. Still, the fact that he was afraid of it happening pissed her off. Like he was some gift to women because of his magical penis.

"Listen, if you have a problem, don't put it on me," she stated, still holding on to her jeans like a shield. "This wasn't what I expected when I left the house this morning, but it definitely got my mind off my problems."

"That's it?" he asked, one brow quirking. "You're glad I could help you push aside your problems for a while? Don't downplay the joys of your first experience."

Strike one to that ego.

"The sex was great. Is that what you want to hear?"

He wrapped an arm around her waist and hauled her body to his. With his free hand he jerked her jeans away and flung them aside. That cool power and confident strength was too damn sexy.

"That's exactly what I want to hear."

Oh, that low tone could get her aroused in less than a second. And he knew it, too.

"We're going to do this again." He slid his mouth back and forth over hers as he spoke. "Whenever I can get you alone again, you'll be mine."

She had to grip his biceps to hold herself upright. "What makes you think I want to do this again?"

Colt eased his hand between them and palmed one

of her breasts. His thumb raked back and forth over her thin bra. "Because I can have you squirming and panting in no time. And because we're not done with each other."

The moment was getting too intense and she needed to regain her composure. She patted the side of his cheek. "I'll let you have sex with me again, but if you go and fall in love, don't say I didn't warn you. I'm quite a catch."

The muscle in his jaw ticked as his eyes dropped to her mouth. She had no clue what was going through his head, but he clearly didn't like the idea of love. Well, that made two of them.

They dressed quietly and found their shirts around the front of the house by the horses. Colt threw her blanket back on Genesis before adjusting the saddle back in place.

As they rode back, all the issues awaiting her flooded her mind. If only life were as perfect as it had been moments ago on the riverbank. Annabelle couldn't even enjoy the euphoria because of the crap storm life had thrown her way.

Since her father was clearly gambling again, she had no idea how she was going to make everything work. He'd ring up more debts, and she'd have to bail him out. That was the cycle and she could only be stretched so thin. She knew gambling, as with any addiction, was a difficult habit to break. But she'd truly hoped losing a daughter and having to borrow money from the neighbor to pay off the mortgage would've slapped some sense into him.

Apparently not.

Annabelle's first priority was making sure Colt got every penny owed to him. She couldn't be her father's keeper and worry about his actions. "Once I get the house paid off, do you think I could continue to work for you until I find something else?"

Putting her pride aside was a bitter pill to swallow. The timing of her question was beyond tacky, but she had no shame at this point. She'd slept with her boss… what was the protocol?

"There's always work to be done on the ranch," he replied easily. "But I figured you'd want to take some time off to be with your girls."

Her girls. Yeah, they were hers. She'd come to think of them as her own and obviously Colt saw that, as well. And sure, in an ideal world where she wasn't broke she could take time off to spend with her family, but these weren't exactly typical circumstances.

"I've got too many bills to take time off."

Silence settled between them before he spoke up again. "Your father is gambling again, isn't he?"

Instantly, tears clogged her throat. She didn't want the world to know her father couldn't keep it together for his family. She despised that he was seen as weak and she resented having to clean up his messes. But the reality was, he had an addiction and she couldn't heal him.

"He took some money from my purse," she muttered, hating how saying those words made her heart ache— hating even more that she had to face the cold reality. "We argued about it this morning."

Great. She'd shared her body with him and now she

felt it necessary to open her heart. She didn't want Colt, or anyone else, to know the details of her father's downfall.

She stole a glance at him, noticing his white-knuckled grip on the reins, the firm set of his jaw.

"Anyway, I've just got more on my plate than I'd hoped for," she went on. "But don't keep me at Pebblebrook out of pity. I'd rather be broke. Besides, I'm sure there are several places in town that are hiring. I worked at an upscale bakery before, so if I could do something along those lines, that would be—"

"You'll stay on at Pebblebrook as long as you want."

His low, commanding tone silenced her. Okay, then. At least that was something. It wasn't the position she dreamed of, but it paid and Colt understood her need to be near Emily and Lucy. If she could just get her bearings and keep her head above water, maybe she'd see the light at the end of the tunnel.

And maybe she'd quit thinking in cheesy clichés, as well.

"Tell me about your brothers," she threw out there. With all the intensity of the day, Annabelle needed normal. Just a simple conversation.

"I know their professions, but why don't they want to be cowboys like you?"

She kept her eyes on the horizon. Pasture as far as the eye could see. In the distance, the tip of the main barn near Colt's house guided their direction.

"Nolan loves the ranch," Colt stated. "He's swamped with the hospital and he's always taking on more shifts. But he helps where he can."

"You have to be pretty proud of what all of your

brothers have accomplished. And I'm sure they're proud of you for keeping all of this running so flawlessly. It's the greatest ranch I've ever seen."

Colt laughed. "I am proud, but it wasn't that long ago you were bashing me and praising them for being nicer and giving back to society."

A sliver of guilt spiraled through her. But, in her defense, that was before she'd developed feelings for Colt.

Oh, no. She was falling for her boss. Was *boss* even the correct term? Landlord? Virginity taker?

Regardless of the label, Annabelle's emotions were calling the shots and now she'd gone and slept with the man. But she wouldn't have been intimate with him if she didn't care for him. And she was starting to care. A lot.

"I think what you've done here at Pebblebrook is amazing."

His thigh brushed against hers as they rode side by side. "I can't take the credit for something my grandfather started and my father carried on."

"No, but you can take credit for keeping up the tradition and loving this land and these animals like they deserve."

She squinted against the sun and tried not to let that random touch throw her off. It was rather difficult to ride back to work like he hadn't just removed her wall of defense and changed her life. No matter what happened at the end of their agreement, or how long she stayed on at Pebblebrook, Colt Elliott would always be her first lover.

"If I owned this land, I'd never want to leave," she added. "It's so peaceful, so perfect."

"That's why I'm here," he told her. "I travel to get away, but I'm always eager to come back home."

As they neared the barn, Annabelle wondered how she was going to be productive when her body still tingled. He'd blatantly told her that their encounter was not a onetime thing. Fine by her because she was more than ready to have that strong body pressed to hers again. When she'd pictured her first experience she'd been married, in a bed, wearing some sexy lingerie she'd purchased for just that occasion.

Instead, she'd been deliciously ravaged on a riverbank before her first cup of coffee.

"I like that smile on your face."

Colt's statement pulled her from her thoughts, and made her realize she had indeed been smiling.

"Makes me think you and I are both having the same thoughts," he added.

"I'm sure we are," she agreed with a slight laugh. "But right now I need to work so I can pay off the rest of my house. So, what are we getting into today?"

Colt's expression sobered. "Actually, I need to run an errand. I'm going to have you take it fairly easy today and clean out the stalls. I'll have Ryan pull down the extra hay from the loft."

"I can do that." How weak did he think she was? "I'm here to work, Colt. Stop coddling me."

He slowed Lightning down, so she pulled Genesis to a stop. When he tipped his hat up and flashed those killer baby blues her way, Annabelle's heart rate sky-rocketed.

Is this how it would be each time he looked at her, now that they'd been intimate?

"I'm not coddling you, sweetness." He reached across and placed his hand high upon her thigh. "I don't want you worn-out because I have plans for you later."

Oh. That promise had her heart in her throat, her body responding. Yes, she was slowly falling for him when she had sworn she wouldn't. Sex clearly had messed with her mind.

"I won't be worn-out," she told him. "I'm sure Ryan has plenty to do without babysitting me and doing part of my job. I've got it covered."

A naughty smile crept over him. "If you're too tired, I guess I'll just get to do all the touching."

"Oh, I won't be that tired, cowboy."

And apparently sex made her a little saucier, too. Who knew?

Fifteen

Once Colt left Annabelle to take care of their horses and get to work, he sent a text to Ryan and Josh to check in on her throughout the day. She wouldn't appreciate it, but too damn bad. He couldn't worry about her and concentrate on this last-minute issue at the same time.

Colt drove a short distance from Pebblebrook and willed himself to calm down. He gripped the wheel, his knuckles turning white. There was too much anger, too much rage and guilt. That last one was on him, but the first two were on another man in Annabelle's life and Colt refused to sit back and watch her have to deal with more pain.

He glanced at the place that would soon be his and the guilt intensified. No, that was the sex talking. He was just feeling the aftershocks of having Annabelle wrapped all around him. He couldn't let those sultry eyes and passion-filled kisses deter him from reaching his goal. He would make sure she had a home, something nice and perfect for her business. But this one was perfect for this business he wanted.

Colt's anger still hadn't eased by the time he pulled up near the porch, but he would keep his head on straight, because Annabelle and her girls were the victims here. Damn it. There was no way not to hurt Annabelle. But he could make the pain less intense.

He rang the doorbell and took a step back. After a minute, Neil Carter opened the old oak door, with the puppy right at his feet. He didn't offer to open the screen—as if that thin partition would keep Colt from business he had with the old man.

"We need to talk," Colt stated.

"Then talk."

He was going to be difficult. Colt didn't know why he thought this would be a simple trip. How could someone as sweet as Annabelle come from someone as cold and self-centered as Neil?

And there went that flare-up of guilt once again. Because Colt knew full well that he was self-centered... otherwise he wouldn't be so dead set on owning this property.

"I'm going to pay off your gambling debts," Colt announced. "Give me the names and contact information. And if I hear of you gambling anymore after that, I'll personally make sure Annabelle knows every last detail of how many times you've borrowed from my family over the years."

Neil crossed his arms over his chest, but before he could utter a word, one of the babies' cries sounded through the house. Neil turned from the door and marched away, the loyal pup on his heels. Colt wasted no time in letting himself inside. With his hand behind him, he caught the screen door before it could slam shut. The anxious puppy turned back around and ran toward Colt, sliding along the hardwood floors and bumping into the toe of his boot.

Colt reached down and petted the little guy and wondered if Annabelle had come up with a name yet. He'd ask her later, but right now, he had some unpleasant business to take care of.

Like any gentleman, Colt removed his hat and hung it on the peg by the door, and then he proceeded to follow the cries into the living room. He walked slowly, careful not to trip or step on the bouncing dog.

Neil picked up one of the girls from some portable pen—Colt believed they were called Pack 'n Plays. They'd both been laying in their side-by-side, chewing on matching pink teethers.

Colt couldn't tell which twin Neil was holding, but he looked closely and thought it might be Lucy. One of them had thicker hair, but that was the only difference he'd noticed. Both girls were like mini-versions of Annabelle.

Lucy continued to whimper, but when she spotted Colt, she reached her arms toward him.

Okay. That was extremely unexpected. He'd held her the other night and fed her, but he didn't realize she'd already know who he was. Neil tossed a glance over his shoulder, reluctant to hand the baby over.

Colt stepped forward and took Lucy from Neil's arms. Her crying ceased as she sniffed and stared at his hair. He figured it was a sweaty mess between his morning activity on the riverbank and riding with his hat on.

"I see you've made an impression on my granddaughter, as well," Neil stated, clearly irritated. "And I don't need you or anyone else to take care of my debts."

"No?" Colt retorted, throwing Neil a sidelong glance. "Because as I see it, your daughter is busting her butt to pay off this house because you couldn't. And when my portion is paid back, she has to continue to work like a dog because she's still trying to save you and now raise twins on top of that."

Colt kept his tone somewhat light because he didn't want to scare the baby. One of her pudgy hands patted the side of his face and Colt couldn't help but smile at her. Those green eyes were going to bring a man to his knees one day.

"I don't need an Elliott taking care of my family," Neil growled. "And whatever you think you're doing with my daughter, she's smarter than to fall for your charms."

Colt wisely kept his opinion on that topic to himself.

"If you would man up, nobody would have to take care of your family."

Colt patted Lucy's back when she laid her head on his shoulder. The innocence of this child humbled him. One day he'd have a baby of his own, raise children on his ranch, and have a wife who shared his passion for the farm. A vision of Annabelle sprang to mind but he quickly vanquished it.

"So far, Annabelle is the only one working toward securing a future for all of you."

Neil's eyes narrowed. "What did she tell you?"

Oh, he wasn't throwing her under the bus. Hell, no. He was there to protect her from all angles...well, except his own agenda. That he couldn't help.

"She didn't have to tell me anything," Colt replied. "I can see how exhausted she is when she comes to the ranch. She gives it her all and then comes here to take care of you guys. There's only so much a person can take before they break and I won't see that happen to her."

"Is that so?" Neil crossed his arms over his chest and shifted his stance. "Why the sudden interest in my Belle? I won't have her hurt."

Something Neil should've thought of before he made the bargain with the Carter ranch and then signed documents he didn't fully read.

"You ever tell her about the jewelry?" Colt threw out.

"No," Neil ground out. "And you don't need to, either. That time has passed. I'm not proud of what I did."

"Passed?" Colt repeated. "You're telling me that you have completely stopped gambling? With no help at all?"

"How do you know I haven't had help?"

Colt merely raised his brows. Lucy's sweet breath tickled the side of his neck. From the steady rhythm, he'd guess she'd fallen asleep. What was it like to be so trusting and innocent?

Annabelle was exactly the same way. She'd trusted the wrong people: her father, her sister, her fiancé... Colt.

"Did you come here to berate me or just rub it in

my face that you've gotten close with my daughter and granddaughters?"

"I came here so you'd realize what you have. You lost one daughter and your other one is here, ready to do anything to make her family work. Is that not enough for you to want to be a better man?"

Neil's lips thinned as he continued to glare at Colt. He didn't care if Neil was pissed, Colt was pretty much boiling since Annabelle had told him her father took money from her purse. Clearly, Neil had an illness, but Annabelle shouldn't have to endure the same struggle. She was trying to restore her life, yet she couldn't even move forward for worry over her father and his ongoing issues.

Damn it. He hadn't planned on getting personally involved. That plan obviously went to hell. Between that kick-ass attitude layered over vulnerability and her loyalty to her family, how could Colt ignore the tug of emotions Annabelle brought to life? But he couldn't allow those emotions to cloud his judgment.

His father had big plans, plans that Colt was to carry out. Colt always made good on his promises. With his father in the nursing facility, there was no way in hell Colt would let him down. Still, that niggle of doubt kept creeping up on him lately. Grant Elliott had always prided himself on being a family man first and foremost. Colt wanted that family life, but he couldn't sacrifice his promise to his father...could he?

If he'd met Annabelle under different circumstances, gotten to know her, date her...but he hadn't. There was nothing but sex between them and when she found out about the legal documents, that would be gone. Even so, Colt would make sure she was taken care of.

Neil closed the distance between them and eased Lucy from Colt's arms. Lucy was indeed fast asleep, while Emily remained fully entertained across the room. Neil cradled Lucy against his chest and stared down at her.

"I'm doing what I can," he murmured. "And after this debt is paid, we won't need your help anymore."

Colt wasn't about to argue. He'd made his point and if Neil didn't want help, then so be it. But that didn't mean Colt wouldn't look out for Annabelle and her babies.

He let himself out the door and climbed back into his truck. He was on borrowed time where Annabelle was concerned. He couldn't go against his family and decades of wishes. Maybe on some level, she would understand that.

Regardless, he wanted her again. He wanted to see her, to touch her. He had a feeling today's workday might just be cut short.

Annabelle swiped the sweat from her forehead with the back of her arm. Ranch life was no joke. No wonder Colt had muscles like that of a calendar model. He'd earned each and every taut bulge.

Finally, the stalls were clean. As if anything in this immaculate barn was ever dirty. Still, she took pride in her position, in the animals. They were such beautiful creatures and deserved to be treated as such.

As she pushed the broom down the stone walkway between the stalls, familiar arms banded around her waist. Instantly she found herself hauled back against a broad chest.

"Sir, I'm working here and there are other employees that could see us."

"Those employees are nowhere near this side of the property and your boss sent me to find you," Colt whispered in her ear. "He said it's time for you to call it a day and meet him at the main house."

Annabelle dropped the broom and turned in his arms. "It's only two o'clock."

Colt shrugged. "Boss's orders, ma'am."

He stepped back and winced slightly. Annabelle reached for him, but he held his hands out.

"It's nothing," he assured her. "I've been riding more than usual and not soaking at the end of the day like I should."

"And you talk about me taking care of myself?"

"Touché."

"Seriously, I need to work. I've only put in about four hours today."

Colt shot her that side grin that never failed to curl her toes. Stupid charming man. Why did she have to be so easily swayed by a dashing smile and a sexy body? Hadn't she learned her lesson the first time a hot guy showed her attention? She'd ended up with his ring on her finger. That incident left her scarred, hollow. But Colt was different. He was loyal to those he cared for.

Never in her life would she have thought that she'd be half in love with an Elliott. Who knows, after this debt was paid off…maybe they could date and see where things went. She wasn't going anywhere and he obviously wasn't, either.

"This will count as a full day's work. You've earned it."

Annabelle reached down to pick up the broom and leaned against it. "Let's say I come up to your house."

"Which you will."

She bit the inside of her cheek to keep from smiling at his confidence, which made him too damn irresistible for his own good. "Let's say that I do. What about Winnie and Charlie? Where are they?"

Colt shrugged. "I'm not positive. I imagine Winnie is in the kitchen preparing some feast for the guys. Charlie is actually out at a ranch in Calhoun County because we're hoping to do some business with them. I sent him because his daughter knows the family there."

Annabelle weighed her options. If her tingly body would shut up, she'd be able to think a little clearer.

"So what do you tell Winnie when I come up to the house and…"

"To my bedroom?" he asked, quirking a dark brow beneath his black hat. "She'd probably throw a party, but to save your reputation, I can sneak you in the back door. She'll never know you're there."

He made things sound so simple, so perfectly tempting. Colt Elliott's bedroom was only a "yes" away and she stood here contemplating her move. What woman did that?

A woman who'd been burned and was falling in love.

Just that morning she'd made some grand speech on

the riverbank, naked as a jaybird, about how she wasn't going to fall for him and he had nothing to worry about.

Liar, liar. It had only been a few hours and she'd analyzed their situation to death. He wanted her land, she wanted him. That pretty much summed up their crazy status in a nice, neat, jam-packed package.

"If you have to think that hard, maybe I didn't do my job earlier today."

Oh, he'd done his job...if his job was to make her fantasize about him all day and watch the opening of the barn for that familiar silhouette. Every time an animal shifted or she heard something, she'd jerked her gaze to that wide-open bay. It was rather schoolgirlish how quickly she'd become infatuated.

Was it the sex? She truly didn't think so. She'd been turned on and intrigued by him since day one, when he'd been nothing but a shirtless stranger.

"Maybe you should show me again just as a reminder," she said, pleased when his bright eyes darkened with arousal.

Good. She wanted to affect him the way he did her. She hoped he thought of her today when they were apart. And, no, she didn't care if that was naive. She had to be honest with herself, if no one else.

"Where did you go today?" she asked.

Colt lifted one broad shoulder. "My day wasn't near as important as my afternoon is about to be."

Sixteen

Colt didn't bring women back to his home, and he sure as hell didn't sneak them through the back door and into his bedroom. The entire third floor made up his domain. He had a balcony off the front and back so he could see the acreage which had been handed down to him...which had been entrusted to him.

So the fact that Annabelle now stood staring out through the back double doors had Colt stilling in the middle of his suite. That long, red hair spiraled down her back. She typically kept it up, but sometime between their morning activities and now, she'd let it all down. He preferred it down, preferred it between his fingers and sliding over his skin.

"I don't know how you ever leave this room in the mornings. I bet the sunrises are amazing."

It was on the tip of his tongue to invite her to see it sometime, but that would require a commitment he couldn't make. Still, he could see it. Annabelle in one of his T-shirts and nothing else, standing just like she was now after a night of lovemaking. He was certain it was an image he would return to long after he revealed the truth and she cut him out of her life for good. Why was that thought becoming more and more agonizing?

Annabelle spun around, her hair dancing about her bare shoulders. She did amazing things to tank tops.

"I should warn you that I've been in horse stalls all day." She wrinkled her nose and damn if it wasn't the most adorable thing he'd ever seen. "I'm not sure what you got into, but you still seem fairly clean, like your deodorant is still working."

Colt laughed. He did that more with her than he had in years. She was unaware of her appeal, she spoke her mind and she was a hard worker. How could a man not find that charming and sexy?

"You're in luck," he told her as he crossed the room. "I happen to love the smell of my ranch."

She rolled her eyes. "You're really a terrible liar."

Actually, he thought he was a stellar one…which was where that guilt kept creeping in from.

He took her hands in his and squeezed, pulling her against his chest. "You're also in luck that I have a shower built for twenty with jetted sprays and three rain heads."

She raised her brows. "A shower? You mean…you're going to shower in the middle of the day?"

"With you," he added, with a smile as her mouth fell

open and her eyes widened. "You need to clean up and I need the heat on my hip. It's a win-win."

"I've never… I mean, that just seems so intimate and…" She narrowed her eyes. "Are you laughing?"

Colt pursed his lips and shook his head. "Not at all."

"Terrible liar," she muttered.

"Then maybe I should use my mouth for more important things."

Before he could ease forward, she took a step back and let go of his hands. "Seriously, Colt. I'm not feeling very attractive right now."

Heat speared him. "You spent the day working on my ranch, tending to my animals. That's the sexiest thing I've seen in a long time."

She tipped her head to the side, her eyes softening. "You take so much pride in this place. It shows."

"It's my life," he stated simply.

When a sadness swept over her features, Colt wasn't having any part of that. Not here, not now, when he wanted her with a need he couldn't even identify.

Reaching behind his back, he jerked his T-shirt up and over his head. There. That's what he wanted to see. Annabelle's eyes locked on his bare torso. Needing to keep her in the moment, he went for his belt buckle.

"If you really want out of those smelly clothes, you could remove them," he suggested.

Her hands shook as she reached for the hem of her tank. Even after this morning she was nervous, or maybe in spite of it. Colt figured she knew exactly what to expect now and fear was getting to her.

Damn it. That was worse than seeing her slip into unhappiness about her current life situation.

"Tell me what you want, sweetheart." He toed off his worn boots and shucked his jeans and boxer briefs. "I'm here for you."

Annabelle finished undressing until she was standing before him just as bare as he was. "I want to see this promised shower that will fulfill my every need."

Colt reached out, snaking an arm around her to pull her into his body. "That would be my job. You have a need, I'll be the one meeting it."

"You might want me to rinse off before you join me," she stated, placing her hands on his shoulders.

Colt turned her toward his bathroom and smacked her rear end. "I'll be the one to wash you, darlin'. Now let's go."

Annabelle's jaw dropped. "This should have another name besides something so simple as a shower."

The walk-in area could indeed hold twenty, she was positive. His bathroom was the size of her entire living room. The all-glass shower with glass tile floor was something from a magazine, as was the rest of his home. How was she ever going to just move on like none of this ever happened?

Colt stepped inside and turned on all the various sprayers. Good grief. Who thought up such necessities? And this was a necessity. She'd give up nearly anything to have a shower like this one.

Annabelle followed him inside and instantly groaned at the glorious heat spraying her from all angles.

"Okay, now I know for sure I'd never leave this room if I lived here. The shower, the view. If I could get food delivered, this would be my very own domain."

"Winnie would be more than happy to—"

She whirled around, shoving her wet hair back from her face. "Winnie will not know I was here in the middle of the day."

Colt laughed as he reached for her. "I'm a bit sore, so you may have to take the lead."

Wrapping her arms around his waist, Annabelle was surprised how easy this felt. How right.

But it wasn't right, was it? He wanted her land, she wanted to fulfill her mother's dream. So they were at a standstill.

"Tell me what to do," she murmured, focusing on the here and now.

Colt grazed his lips along her jawline and up to her ear. "Listen to what your body wants. I guarantee it will match what mine is telling me."

She went up onto her toes to kiss him. Curling her fingers around his shoulders, she backed him toward the bench running along the back wall. His mouth devoured hers and it was all she could do not to climb all over him.

Everything between them had escalated at an alarming speed, but she couldn't stop...didn't want to stop. Colt had becoming a craving and she wasn't going to deprive herself. She deserved happiness, even if it was only temporary.

Annabelle eased her mouth away and pushed on Colt's shoulders, silently urging him to have a seat. As he sat, he raked his hands down her sides, grazing her breasts as he went.

She stepped back out of his reach and glanced around. She spotted the soap and shampoo on the built-in shelf on the adjacent wall. An idea sparked and then fully engulfed her mind. She was going to be daring and seductive, she hoped. If she could drive him out of his mind half as much as he had done to her, this afternoon shower session would be a success.

Annabelle grabbed the shampoo and squirted some into her hand. As she lathered her hair, she made sure to get a good arch in her back, thrusting her chest in Colt's direction…and she was pretty sure she'd heard a groan escape him.

Tipping her head back, she rinsed the shampoo away, suds gliding down her body. She shot him a wink and a smile as she went back for the soap. With no washcloth in sight, she squeezed some soap into her hands and lathered them up before sliding it over her arms, her legs, her torso.

Each slow stroke was like torture. She wanted his hands on her, but the way he was squirming on that bench, his piercing gaze locked on her every move, Annabelle knew it was only a matter of time before he snapped.

Anticipation flooded her.

"Enough."

Colt's harsh demand had Annabelle jerking around to face him fully. His body was tight, shoulders squared, jaw set, and those eyes held hers as if he'd reached out and touched her.

"Come here."

Water hit her from all around as she made her way back across the shower. Annabelle came to stand between his legs, and his hands instantly gripped her waist.

"I think you're clean enough for what I have in mind."

Arousal spiraled low in her belly.

"I didn't bring any protection in here with me," he told her. "But I've never gone without and I guarantee I'm clean."

Even though she'd been a virgin up until this morning, she'd been on birth control since she was twenty.

"I'm safe," she assured him.

His eyes darkened as he raked them over her bare chest, her torso, between her thighs. As his gaze traveled back up, she shivered and braced her hands on his shoulders. Colt urged her forward and she placed her knees on either side of his hips.

"I want nothing between us," he muttered.

Slowly, Annabelle joined their bodies. At the onslaught of sensations, her head fell back. Colt reached around, gripping her wet hair and pulling just enough. Her body went into action as she couldn't stay still another second.

As he tugged on her hair, his mouth closed over one breast and Annabelle didn't know how long she could hold out. The sprays hit her from the back, the side, and Colt's hands and mouth were assaulting her in the most delicious ways.

"That's it," he urged.

Apparently he knew her body better than she did because she instantly tightened around him as pleasure tore through her.

Colt flattened his palms against her back, captured her mouth and crushed her entire body against him as if he wanted to completely absorb her. The tip of his tongue parted her lips, and everything inside Annabelle exploded. Colt stiffened beneath her as he tore his mouth away and rested his forehead to hers. His fingertips dug into her back as his own release consumed him.

Moments later, when the trembling had ceased and the water continued to caress them, Annabelle kept her eyes closed. She didn't want to face reality. She didn't want Colt to look in her eyes because of what he'd see. She'd fallen for him. Completely. She had no idea how she would continue to work for him and keep this secret.

But she had no choice. They were on opposite ends of life's spectrum and he'd made it clear that this was nothing more than sex. Too bad her heart didn't get that memo.

Seventeen

"I was engaged before." Colt laid that declaration between them as they dressed after the shower. "You're the only other woman I've ever had in this house."

Annabelle squeezed her hair into a plush towel, but her eyes remained on his. "I didn't think you were a monk, Colt. Besides, this is just physical, right? I don't need to know your history."

Wearing only his jeans, Colt crossed the spacious bathroom until he stood before her. He pulled the towel from her hands, grasped her hair, and proceeded to rub the dripping ends of crimson.

"I believe we both know this escalated into more than just sex." As much as he didn't want it to, and as much as these damn emotions complicated everything, there was no denying the fact that Annabelle had gotten to him. "I don't know what to call it, or if we even need a label, but I like being with you even outside the bedroom."

"Like on a riverbank?" she asked, a half smile curving over her swollen lips.

Tossing the towel aside, he curled his fingers around the back of her neck and brought his forehead to hers. "Everywhere. I like you in my barns, on my horses, the way you look at my land. I just, I don't know how to explain it all."

Annabelle looped her arms around his neck. "I've only really known you for less than a week," she stated. "I knew Matt for a year, was engaged to him, but I never felt like this."

His ego, which she'd claimed was inflated, grew even more at her words. Warmth spread through him, knowing that there was a strong undercurrent of emotions running through her, as well. But how the hell did he go about this without totally screwing everything up? How did he keep the land and the woman once all was said and done?

Maybe she never had to know about the documents. Perhaps now that their connection was growing deeper, he could use that momentum.

This was crazy. One of the most reckless decisions he'd ever made, but in order to have it all, it was his only option.

Colt framed her face, tipping her head up so he could see those gorgeous green eyes. "Move in with me."

Her chest pressed against his as she pulled in a gasp.

That unpainted mouth dropped into a perfect O. He wasn't going to give her a chance to turn him down.

"You can take your time finding a job you like or keep working at Pebblebrook," he went on. "I don't care. But I want you here in my house, in my bed."

"But…but I have six-month-old twins," she muttered, as if thinking aloud of reasons she shouldn't agree.

"I didn't expect you to come alone. There's even plenty of room for your dad if he wants to join us. I have eight bedrooms on the second floor. The master is plenty large enough for cribs."

What was he saying? Was he really willing to play house to ensure that her land remained his and she would never know what he'd done?

Yes. And in his defense, some of his motives were completely selfish, but he truly wanted to spare Annabelle any more hurt. She'd been through so much, too much, and all at the hands of people she'd trusted.

And she trusted him with the most important aspect of her life. No way could he betray her now. Seeing her in pain, knowing he'd caused it, would be like a knife to his heart.

She closed her eyes and blew out a sigh. "Colt, this is all so much to take in. I don't trust my feelings right now."

Colt took her hand, placed it over his bare chest and flattened it with his own. "You feel me, feel us. I'm not asking for anything more than you to live here and give this a shot."

"I'm adjusting from so much," she whispered, tears pricking her eyes. "I lost my sister, a man I thought I trusted. My finances are a joke and I'm learning how to be a mom."

"All the more reason for you to come here. Finances will never be an issue." Colt would make it his personal mission to keep her father out of trouble. "And Winnie would be happy to help you care for the girls. In fact, she'd love it."

"And you?" she asked, her eyes hopeful.

"I've always wanted a family and kids." That was absolutely true. He just never thought they'd land in his path like this. "This place was made for children."

"You want kids of your own?" she asked, then shook her head. "That was a silly question. You asked me to move in, not bear your children."

An image of her pregnant with his baby ripped something open in him. Yeah, he did want children and if he had them with Annabelle, he knew they'd be strong-willed, independent kids who could take on the ranch in the years to come.

Was he...no. He wasn't falling in love. Was he?

He'd vowed to keep deeper emotions separate, but that simply wasn't possible anymore. Still, she couldn't find out about the paperwork her father signed. Colt refused to be the one to destroy her life once again.

"I don't want to get hurt."

She blinked back her tears, and Colt knew in that moment, he'd do anything to keep her safe.

And he also knew then that he had fallen for her. How had this happened? Within days he'd gone on such a roller coaster ride of emotions with her, Colt didn't know when his control had started to slip.

Perhaps all of his power transferred over to her the moment she plowed into the fence and stared at him as if she wanted to mount him right in his driveway. Because from the start, Annabelle had held the proverbial reins. She'd pulled him into her world and he knew now that he wanted to stay.

"If you need to think about it, that's fine," he told her, knowing someone like Annabelle didn't make rash decisions. "I'm not going anywhere."

"I need to pay off my father's debt," she told him. "How would we work that out? I mean, I'd feel a little weird paying you and sleeping in your bed. Assuming that's where you'd want me."

Colt wrapped his arms around her waist, filling his hands with her backside. "My bed is the only option for you."

When she went up onto her toes and covered his lips with her own, Colt knew she'd already made her decision. She may not have voiced it yet, but she would.

He would have everything he wanted and nobody had to get hurt. A burst of relief spread through him as he captured her lips, but a shrill ring from the bedroom broke the moment.

Annabelle pulled away and rushed in to answer the call. Colt grabbed his shirt and pulled it over his head.

"I'll be right there."

He noticed Annabelle's worried tone as she slid the cell into her pocket. "I have to go," she told him.

"What's wrong? Is it the girls?"

She shook her head, glancing around the room for her boots. Pulling one from beneath the bed skirt and one from the other side of the bed, she hopped on one foot then the other to pull them on.

"Dad didn't say. He just said he needed me home right now."

Fear pushed through him as he grabbed his own phone from his dresser and followed her out of the bedroom. They hurried out the back door of the house, just the same way they'd come in. Silence accompanied them as he drove her back home in his truck.

Colt had barely pulled to a stop in front of her porch when he recognized the silver SUV in the drive. His heart sank.

"Annabelle, wait."

But she was already out of his truck and running toward the door. That future he'd just secured only moments ago in his bedroom was about to blow up in his face.

And that vow to keep Annabelle from getting hurt by his actions? Well, he was getting a front row seat to an epic debacle and there wasn't a damn thing he could do about it.

"What's wrong?" Annabelle asked the second she stepped through the front door. "Where are the babies?"

She took in so much at once. Her father stood in the middle of the foyer with a stranger. The puppy was bouncing between everyone like he'd just found new friends.

"I just laid them down for a nap," her father replied. "It seems this engineer was hired by Colt to do some work on the house."

"I'm only here to take a quick look around," the stranger replied as he turned his attention toward her. "My name is Sam Stevens. I work for the Elliott family. They gave me this address and I just came to do a quick survey. I wasn't aware people were living here."

Confusion settled deep as she tried to grasp what was happening. And all of this was on the coattails of Colt asking her to move in with him.

Annabelle crossed her arms over her chest and addressed Sam. "What exactly did Colt ask you to do here?"

The engineer had a clipboard in his hand and held it up for her to see a long list of items. "Various renovations. But I can come back at a better time."

"We don't need you to come back," Neil chimed in. "I'll take care of this."

Annabelle turned to see Colt standing in the doorway. She was still perplexed at why this man was here, but the guilt written on Colt's face painted a clearer picture.

"Sorry, Mr. Elliott." Sam tapped the clipboard against his side, drawing the puppy over to his feet. "When we talked the other day, I figured you were ready to move forward with this project so I wanted to come out and get your estimate—"

Colt held up a hand, cutting the man off. "I appreciate your work. But for now, let me handle this. I'll be in touch."

Annabelle watched as the engineer nodded obediently, then sent her and her father an apologetic smile.

Once he was gone, her father scooped up the rambunctious pup.

"Let me put him out back and then I want to know what the hell you're doing, Elliott."

Annabelle watched her father walk away, not wanting to glance back to Colt. She didn't want to know the truth, didn't want her fears to come to life. Surely he wasn't the monster she was imagining right at that moment.

"Darlin'," he began.

She held up a hand. "No. Don't start that. Tell me what that man was doing in *my* house."

The muscle in his jaw ticked as he raked a hand over the back of his neck. His hair was still damp from their shower, as was hers. She jerked the band from her wrist and pulled her hair back into a loose bun. Only a short time ago she was in his arms, coming apart, and then he was opening up to her about his feelings, his hopes for a future with her.

And now he stood before her a total stranger.

"Sam works for me."

"We got that," her father said, coming back to stand next to Annabelle. "What the hell was he doing here on your orders?"

Annabelle watched as Colt waged a war with himself. Her stomach tightened as she leaned against the banister on the staircase for support. She met his gaze from across the foyer. "The truth, Colt."

"I was going to have some work done on the house to get it up to the standards I needed."

A piece of her heart broke, fell at her feet and shattered.

"Because?" she asked, thick emotions welling up in her throat.

"Because this house is going to be part of my dude ranch."

"The hell you say?" Her father was on the verge of exploding. "I paid off my loan to the bank and this house is mine."

Colt cleared his throat, his chest puffed out as he drew in a breath. "Actually, the house and the land belong to me."

"What?" Annabelle gasped. "How is that possible? I've worked myself to death for the payments coming due."

Honestly, she didn't want to know the answer. He'd deceived her. He'd lied to her face, made a joke of her and she'd given him her virginity. How naive could she be?

Baby cries echoed over the baby monitor in the living room. She'd come to tell them apart and this was definitely Emily. Annabelle turned toward the steps, but her father held up a hand.

"I'll go." He threw a glance to Colt before turning back to her. "See what this mess is all about."

Once they were alone again, Annabelle sank onto the steps. The fight was leaving her. She'd been hit so hard, so often lately, she wasn't sure she could keep standing for the final knockout.

"Just tell me," she stated as she wrapped her arms around her knees.

"I want to explain why—"

"No." Annabelle held up her hand. "I don't care about

the why. That part is obvious. You're a selfish bastard, only looking out for your family, your precious land and not caring who you hurt in the process."

"Yes. That was the case at first. But then you came into the picture."

Annabelle laughed. "Seriously? That's the route you're going to take for the defense? You were dead set on having my childhood home, but then you saw me and the error of your ways shone bright. Am I close?"

Suddenly she felt like fighting. The burst of anger surged her to her feet. It felt good, and kept the hurt at bay. "So let's hear it. How do you own this? Because when you gave Dad the money, he paid the bank. Now we owe you and he signed a paper with you… Oh, no. What did he sign?"

Any minute she'd wake from this nightmare.

Colt took a step toward her, but she held out both hands. Emily's cries echoed once again over the monitor, along with her father's soothing words. This house meant everything to her and she wasn't about to let Colt take it away. Surely there was something she could do.

"When he asked for the money to pay off the loan, I offered to buy the place for more than market value, all cash. He turned me down. So when I gave him the money to pay off the loan, I had everything put in writing. My attorney drew up a document stating the amount due back and how it should be split into payments."

Annabelle shook her head. "Wait. Why would Dad come to you for the money anyway? I've wondered that from the beginning."

When he hesitated and glanced away, she threw her

arm in the air. "Oh, come on. It's a little late to protect me now, isn't it? You've taken everything from me, just say it."

Colt dropped his head between his shoulders and stared down at his worn boots. "That's not the first time I've loaned him money."

She couldn't have heard him right. "What?"

"He's borrowed before," Colt stated, bringing his bright gaze up to hers.

"And...has he paid you back?" she whispered.

Colt shook his head. "That's how I knew I could have this place. He was so desperate for the money, he didn't read what he signed. It states that after the debt is paid back to me, I will be the sole owner of your property, the house, and all outbuildings."

The wind literally was knocked out of her as if he'd punched her in the gut. She reached out, placing a hand on the newel post, and looked out the window toward the large oak tree in the front yard.

How could this day be so bright and sunny when inside her heart was black and stormy? There was nothing left. She literally had nothing but a gambling father and two babies depending on her.

"Annabelle."

"Don't say my name. Don't talk to me and don't ever touch me again." She jerked and took a step backward. "You made a fool of me. You used me on your ranch, worked me like one of your minions, purposely seduced me and made me feel... I hate you for that most of all."

Dampness tickled her cheeks, and she swiped the

backs of her hands across her face. "Get out. Get the hell out so I can figure out what to do now."

The harsh reality slapped her in the face. "I can't order you out of your own house, can I? Damn it. Can you at least give us a few days to find someplace to go? We need to pack…and my mother's things are in the attic…her dishes, where will I store all of that?"

She was thinking out loud, muttering really, because she certainly wasn't talking to the devil disguised as a cowboy.

"You can stay here," he told her. "I wasn't going to just kick you out. I will buy you someplace to stay. You can pick it out."

Tears flooded down her cheeks and she didn't even care at this point. Pride be damned. She had nothing left to lose.

"I don't want a thing from you," she growled. "I don't ever want to see your face again. I don't want to hear your name. We'll be out by Friday. Tell your precious engineer he can return then."

He continued to stare at her, and she had to be hallucinating because she could've sworn she saw pain in his eyes. But men with cold hearts and no souls didn't hurt.

"Everything that happened between us was real," he told her. "I have feelings for you and I wanted you to move in so we could try—"

"So I wouldn't find out what a lying jerk you are?" she asked, another realization hitting her square in the chest. "My eyes are wide-open now. You only wanted me at Pebblebrook so I wouldn't learn the truth. But you got your wires crossed with one of your minions, exposing you for the worthless man you are."

Why did looking at him hurt so badly? Those blue eyes that had captivated her for days, held her when they made love…

No. They hadn't made love. They'd acted on their attraction and used each other for sex. Nothing more. No matter how much she thought she'd been in love with him.

"I care for you," he told her, and his tone might have been convincing had she not known the truth. "I want you happy, I want to help your family. Let me find you another house."

A humorless laugh escaped her. "I'd think you of all people would understand the importance of family tradition and loyalty. I don't want another place and I most definitely don't want you paying for it. I'd live on the street before I took a dollar from you."

It may come to that. But she'd figure something out. An inexpensive apartment in town could always serve as backup.

"Annabelle—"

"Leave, Colt. You've got the house, the land. That's what you wanted, right?" She bit down on her quivering lip and swallowed. "You have everything now."

His eyes misted. "Not everything."

Then he was gone, leaving Annabelle to sink back to the steps. After all the fighting, all the hurdles she'd jumped, she had been defeated by a man she'd fallen for in a whirlwind affair.

Her broken heart would have to wait. Right now, she had a house to pack and a future to try to piece back together…a future without any dream coming true.

Eighteen

Colt slammed his office door and cursed the moment he'd decided to back Neil Carter into a corner.

The land was his. The debt wasn't fully paid, but the end result was inevitable since Neil signed the papers. For years Colt had dreamed of this moment. He'd waited for the day when he could tell his father that they had secured the land next door and were ready to move forward with Pebblebrook Dude Ranch. The extra home and barns would be useful space. Added to that, the other property carved into the corner of Pebblebrook and now their ranch would be complete.

But instead of texting his brothers the news or rushing to the nursing home to tell his father, Colt went straight to his bar and poured himself a tumbler of bourbon. He downed it, welcoming the familiar burn.

Getting drunk wouldn't solve a thing. It sure as hell wouldn't turn back the clock and give him the chance to handle this whole ordeal differently.

But he truly didn't know what he'd change. He wanted the land, that was obvious. Hurting Annabelle was never part of the deal. She'd come to him broken, ready to slay any dragon in her way to save her family. He'd admired her from day one and had instantly set out on claiming her.

Well, he'd done that, as well. So now what? He had the land, he'd slept with Annabelle, and now she held his heart. How the hell did he get himself into this mess and how could he work his way back out without doing more damage?

Damn it. He hadn't expected emotions to botch up the triumph of his success.

His office door jerked open and Colt barely raised his gaze to his brother in the doorway.

"Not in the mood," Colt growled as he poured another round. Nothing like toasting your failures with yourself and having your oldest brother, the miracle surgeon, as a witness.

"I saw you tear in here like your world just ended." Nolan didn't take the not-so-subtle hint that Colt wanted to be alone. He crossed the office and stopped on the other side of the bar. "I assume this has to do with Annabelle."

Colt tipped back the glass and closed his eyes before slamming the empty tumbler back onto the mahogany bar top.

"The land is ours and the engineer will be moving

forward with drawing up some plans and getting us an estimate."

Nolan braced his hands against the grooved edge of the bar and leaned forward. "Which is what you've always wanted, so I'm assuming Annabelle knows that she no longer has a home."

"She knows everything."

Well, not everything. There was one more thing he could do for her that might lessen her pain. She'd still hate him, he couldn't change that, but he owed her.

"You care for her." Nolan let out a low whistle. "I didn't see that coming. But I can tell you from experience, if you want to be with her, fight. No matter what you've done, you can't let her go."

Colt shook his head. "She doesn't ever want to see me or talk to me again. Those were her parting words."

"And you're just giving up? You fought for years for this property, but when you find a woman you care for you opt to drink and will the pain away?"

Wasn't that what any cowboy did?

"She deserves for you to grovel, to show her that she means more than this dream of yours," Nolan went on. "But only if she does mean more. I could be reading you all wrong, but you look like hell."

Colt had never second-guessed a business decision he'd made. Confidence was key to maintaining a successful ranch. But right now, he wanted this pain to go away. And he knew if he was hurting this much, that Annabelle was miserable. She was still trying to pick up the pieces of her shattered life and all he'd done was throw more shards into the mix.

"There's no fixing this," Colt stated, pushing away from the bar. "I can make the process a little easier, but she doesn't want my help. I offered to buy her another house."

Nolan laughed and raked a hand through his dark hair. "You don't get women at all, man. She doesn't want another house. She wants the one she grew up in. We don't need that property to grow, Colt. We have five thousand acres. Use some of the east side to build cabins. You want the girl, go get her. If you're content with simply keeping the property, stay here and drink your day away."

Nolan started back toward the door before stopping and glancing over his shoulder. "Don't make the same mistake I did."

Colt knew Annabelle didn't want to see him. He needed to give her time before he approached her again and explained his side, and maybe then she'd understand.

But if he wanted to nudge her in the right direction, then he needed to take something to her, something that rightfully belonged to her.

There was no denying the truth any longer...he loved Annabelle. In a short time, she'd captured his heart. Oh, she'd fought the attraction, but he'd pursued her and he wasn't sorry. How could he be? She was the greatest thing that had happened to him and he'd destroyed their chance at happiness before it could even get started.

He had to prove to her that he wasn't an unfeeling jerk.

Colt headed to his master suite to retrieve the box he'd had hidden for nearly two years. Doing the right thing at this point was rather moot, but he couldn't let Annabelle believe he was the monster she claimed.

* * *

"I'm sorry, Belle."

If she only had a dollar for every time her father had said those words just this evening alone…

Annabelle cradled a sleepy Emily and swayed back and forth on the porch. "There's nothing we can do now. We wouldn't have the money to fight that document anyway. But I am going to demand to see it. I know Colt wouldn't have allowed for any loopholes, but I won't take his word for it."

From the start, she'd known he had an agenda, but she'd thought most of it was getting her into bed. She had a clue he wanted her land, but she never dreamed he already owned it.

She heated all over again when she thought of how foolish she was, how much of a laughingstock she must've been each time she showed up for so-called work at the ranch.

From here on out, she was focusing on her girls. Annabelle needed to go out first thing in the morning and find a job, and then she'd look into housing.

The thought of packing up the only place she'd ever wanted to be hurt almost as much as Colt's betrayal. Just his name in her mind had her heart aching.

"We'll get through this," she told her father. "But when I say no gambling, I mean it. This can't go on. I don't care if it's one dollar or one hundred. No more."

He stood up from the swing, sending it rocking on its own in the breeze. "I'm going to do everything I can. I know we need to do this together. I'm trying."

"I know." He was always trying, but this time he had

to stick to a plan and now that she was back, maybe she could watch him more closely. "Go on to bed," she told him. "I'll come in later. I just want to hold her a while longer and enjoy the silence and the fresh air."

She wanted to sit on this porch swing with Emily and Lucy, just like her mother used to do with Annabelle and her sister. Leaving the memories behind would be the hardest part. Seeing the inside of this home bare would quite possibly break her.

"I can take Emily in and lay her down if you'd like. It's rather late."

Annabelle nodded. "I know, but she can sleep in my arms. She calms me, gives me peace. I guess I'll have that time to spend with my babies after all until I find another job."

Considering the hell she'd been through, Annabelle needed peace. She needed to focus on her family, on piecing the broken hearts back together.

"We're going to rebuild our lives," he told her. "With your mother and Trish gone…"

His voice caught and it was all Annabelle could do to hold it together. Her father never broke down in front of her.

"Now that they're gone," he said on a shaky breath. "You are all I have. You and those sweet girls. I want to be a better man for you guys and I want you to know I'm going to help by getting a job. We'll do this together."

She truly hoped so because she wasn't sure she could do it alone. "I love you, Dad."

He crossed to her, kissed the top of her head, and headed inside. Annabelle patted Emily through the cotton sleeper and made her way to the swing. Wherever she ended up, Annabelle vowed to own a porch with a swing. It may not be this porch, it may not be this swing, but it was a tradition she could take with her.

Tears slid down her cheeks as she pushed off the porch with her toes to set the swing in motion again. Emily clutched onto Annabelle's T-shirt as she drifted off to sleep. Trish's precious babies were counting on her to provide protection, stability, a future, and she planned to deliver.

So much had happened today and Annabelle was still trying to wrap her mind around the fact that she was still in love with a man who had hurt her so deeply, she didn't know if she'd ever recover.

But he'd told her all along that family was everything to him. He hadn't been lying.

He'd cradled her in his arms after making love and told her his father's ultimate goal when he'd been in charge. Now Colt was pushing forward with those plans no matter who was run over in the process. A part of her knew where he was coming from, realized the importance of clinging to a parent's dream.

Still, it didn't cancel out what he'd done. He'd stolen her home. From the moment she met him, he knew exactly what the outcome of this situation would be and he chose to play with her life anyway. Those actions were unforgivable.

Headlights swept up her driveway and Annabelle came to her feet, tightening her hold on Emily and pulling her into her chest.

Colt's truck came to a stop and Annabelle braced

herself. If he was coming to beg for forgiveness, he could take his shiny, expensive vehicle and get the hell off her...

It was his land. He had every right to be there.

The soft glow from the porch cast enough light for her to see that he was carrying a box. As he drew closer, she recognized that box. Her mother's.

Annabelle went to the edge of the porch and met his eyes when he stopped at the base of the steps.

"I'm not staying," he told her. "I just thought this should be returned to you."

There was no holding back the tears, making it difficult to juggle a sleeping baby while swiping at her eyes with the back of her hand.

"Why do you have my mother's jewelry box?"

Colt held the box between his hands, his attention never wavering from her. "Because your father needed money. He knew there wasn't anyone around who could afford to buy this, so he came to me."

She'd known her father had sold the jewelry, but she hadn't known to whom and she never dreamed she'd get it back.

"Is it all in there?" she dared ask.

"Every piece," he confirmed. "I had no use for it. I always figured if Neil got straightened out, he may want this back. But you deserve it."

She didn't know what to say. He could've kept this box and she never would've known. Clearly, her father wasn't going to say anything.

Annabelle stepped aside. "Can you set it on the table over there?" she asked.

Colt stepped up onto the porch and placed the box on the side table next to a rocking chair and potted fern. The breeze kicked up, bringing Colt's familiar woodsy scent with it. The same scent she'd been up close and personal with in his shower earlier.

When he turned back around and locked his eyes on hers, Annabelle froze. "Don't," she whispered.

"I know you hate me. I know you think I'm the worst person you've ever met."

In the pale glow, those blue eyes glistened with unshed tears. She didn't want to believe he had a heart. She didn't want him to have feelings. He'd done all this to himself, to her and her family.

"But everything that happened with us was real. I didn't want it to be," he added. "I wanted to keep things business and physical. You showed me there was so much more. I know you don't believe me, but I had to tell you that I'm not the man you think. I'm just a guy who put his father's wishes above all else. I'm a guy who wanted to prove himself to those people he loved most."

Colt pursed his lips, but Annabelle didn't miss the way his chin quivered. Her heart ached for him, but again, she hadn't done any of this. All of his pain was self-inflicted.

"And in the end, I hurt the woman I'd fallen in love with."

Annabelle had barely processed the words when he turned and walked off the porch. That limp, a little more prominent this evening, only reminded her that he was human. That he made mistakes, he wasn't perfect. But he'd hurt her and now he just wanted to turn her world on its side once again with those words?

She clutched Emily and turned, going down the steps.

"You can't drop that bomb so conveniently and then just leave," she called.

"Too late. But there's little I can do to make you believe me," he told her as he opened the truck door. "I just want you to know…"

He shook his head and glanced toward the starry sky before looking back at her. "I just want you to know that those moments I spent alone with you were some of the best of my life."

Colt hopped into the cab of his truck and backed away, not looking in her direction again. Emily slept through the entire encounter and Annabelle envied her for it.

Colt had brought back her mother's box, the box Annabelle remembered playing with as a little girl. Oh, there were plenty of real pieces in there, but her mom had also kept costume jewelry, too.

Annabelle sat in the rocker beside the box and nestled Emily into the crook of her arm. With her free hand, Annabelle lifted the lid and was instantly swept back in time. The emerald earrings that matched the ring Annabelle had were safely in their divider.

All of the other familiar pieces were there, too. Memories of her mother wearing each one came rushing back.

Closing her eyes, she rested her head against the back of the rocker and longed for answers. What was she supposed to do? How could she move on when it would be so easy to give up?

And how did she process Colt's announcement that he'd fallen for her? That wasn't fair. She wanted to continue hating him, but he'd sounded sincere. Those tears he blinked away were certainly not fake, but how could he feel that way about her and still treat her like he had?

Unless…

Annabelle needed to think. She needed to clear her head and dissect all that had transpired in the past few months. She couldn't just do what her heart told her to because there was no way she was following that advice anymore.

She had to be smart about this and make the best decisions for her and the twins. And that started with marching over to Pebblebrook first thing in the morning.

Nineteen

Hard work made a man forget, or at least that's what he'd told himself when he came to the barn at five that morning.

Colt had intentions of working until his muscles burned and he temporarily forgot how much his heart ached. He'd only meant to take that box to Annabelle last night, but then he'd seen her holding Emily and his mouth just opened, pouring emotions out.

And in that moment his future became so clear. Family, above all else, was the most important thing in life. His father had never put anything above his family... not even business. The Elliotts were all successful because they'd put integrity and loyalty first.

Annabelle may still hate him, but he wasn't giving up. He may have been determined to get her farm, but that was nothing compared to the motive he had to get her back. She was…everything. She was absolutely everything he'd ever wanted and he hadn't even known it.

Colt had texted Ryan and Josh, telling them to start work on the west side near Hayes's house. Not only did Colt want that place perfect for his brother's return in a few weeks, but he wanted the guys away because he was not in the mood for chitchat.

He'd taken Lightning out first thing and tried to clear his mind, but all he kept seeing was the hurt on Annabelle's face when she realized he'd lied to her. He'd not only lied, he'd stolen the one thing she'd held dear to her heart since she was a child.

As soon as he'd come back from his ride, Colt had gone straight into his office in the barn and fired off an email. He may never get Annabelle back, but he sure as hell wasn't about to continue the process of taking her home.

Guilt had gnawed at him into the wee hours. But there was so much more. That moment on Annabelle's porch last night had turned the final click on his heart, proving that he didn't only love her, he loved the image of her and those babies being his, living on Pebblebrook.

He loved her more than he'd thought possible and had completely crushed her.

All his own doing and his brother tried to tell him. Hell, his employees had, too.

But Colt had been stubborn. Now he'd have to do damage control. His father wouldn't have approved of Colt letting the woman go only to have the expansion. His father would be disappointed in how Colt had handled everything. But that wasn't the only reason Colt decided to fight for what he wanted.

A car door slamming caught his attention as he tossed another bale of hay from one side of the loft toward the opening near the ladder.

Stepping over hay, he crossed to the small hinged door and swung it open wide. Glancing down, he saw the most beautiful sight: Annabelle in a pair of fitted jeans, a green tank that matched her eyes and her boots. She pulled a stroller out of the trunk and slammed the lid. Then she opened the back door and removed Emily and Lucy from their car seats.

He watched as she strapped them into the stroller and then looked around the open area. She was there to see him, but why? Had his words affected her last night? Was she willing to hear him out and maybe start over?

He hadn't had a chance to rehearse his speech in his head. He wasn't ready to face her when his emotions were so raw and vulnerable. But there was nothing more he wanted than to believe she came there to forgive him.

He was asking too much, he knew, but he still wasn't ready to give up. Maybe spouting off his profession of love last night had been wrong, but if it got her thinking, he wasn't sorry he'd exposed his weaker side.

"Up here," he called.

Annabelle jumped, a hand over her heart as she glanced toward him. Her eyes landed on his bare chest. "Oh, um… I need to talk to you."

"I'll come down."

He didn't bother to grab his shirt from the hayloft. It had been hot as Hades up there so he'd shed it early. As

Colt climbed down the ladder, he didn't care that he was playing dirty by going at her half-dressed. He'd do anything to remind her of just how good they were together.

"I want to see that document my father signed."

He'd barely put his boot on the ground when she came up the walkway pushing the twins. The girls were bright eyed today and Lucy was chewing on some stuffed cowboy doll. The sight of those expressive green eyes clutched his heart.

He focused back on Annabelle. "I have the print copy in my office at the house."

She nodded. "Then let's go there."

"We can go into my office here and I can pull up the document in email format that I sent to my attorney."

She kept trying to look him in the eye, but she failed. Every few seconds her focus shifted down to his bare chest.

"That's fine. I want to know what I'm dealing with and if there's any way to get out of it."

"The document is binding, darlin'."

"Do not even start with that," she told him, her eyes now locked on his. "I want to know something and I want you to answer honestly."

He crossed his arms and nodded. "I have nothing else to hide."

She gripped the handles of the stroller and tipped her head. "When you asked me to move in with you, was that because you wanted me or because you were trying to cover your tracks so I wouldn't find out about the property? I assume you were hoping I'd fall madly in love with you and we'd just merge and live happily ever after. Am I right?"

Colt swallowed. "Yes."

When she lowered her lids over those mesmerizing green eyes, Colt felt as if the day had dimmed. Her light was gone and he'd put it out. He had to explain himself and then she could decide what to do.

"I asked you to move in because I was serious about wanting to try for something deeper with you." He took a step closer. "I asked because if you fell in love with me and we did this whole happily-ever-after, then you'd never have to know what your father or I did." Another step brought him toe to toe with her. "But I wanted to spare you the pain, I wanted you to start a new life without the heartache. The last thing I ever wanted was to hurt you."

She opened her eyes, tilting her head so she could meet his gaze. "You didn't want to hurt me? What did you think would happen? Did you seriously think I'd never find out about this form my father signed?"

Colt watched as Emily turned the toy over again, then put it back in her mouth. "After I started falling for you, I did what I could to keep you safe. I wanted to protect you. I was trying to find a way to keep my father's wishes and hold on to you at the same time. What I didn't realize was that my father would rather see me happy and settled than to have the extra land for the dude ranch."

"How can I believe you?" she whispered.

She was breaking down. Now all he had to do was catch her.

"Because this place is better with you. Because my life is brighter with you here. I've always wanted a family and the moment I held Lucy out in the yard, I started falling. I had a weak spot for you, and getting to know your girls more only made the trio even more appealing. I want you all here, Annabelle."

She'd left her hair down today. The soft curls lay over her shoulders and he remembered the deep shade of red her hair turned when wet. He'd give anything to have her back in his shower again, in his bed, in his life.

"I messed up," he went on. "I'll freely admit that I should've been honest with you from the moment you came, but I didn't know you and I only wanted to fulfill my father's wishes... I guess the same as you did with your mother."

Annabelle's soft smile clenched his heart. "That bed-and-breakfast was her only goal."

"Then you can do it," he told her. "Take your house and do whatever you want with it."

Her brows drew in. "What?"

"I emailed my attorney this morning regarding the legal agreement. It will be reversed and the land will remain in your name."

Emily started fussing and threw her toy on the ground. Colt picked up the cowboy as Annabelle came around to lift the baby from the stroller. With Emily on her hip, Annabelle turned to face him once again.

"Why?" she asked simply.

Colt shrugged and held the toy up to Emily. "Because it's yours. I only want you and if I can't have you, then I sure as hell don't want to take your home."

There was an emptiness inside him that had existed since he left her house last night. He needed it filled, but only Annabelle had that power.

"You're just giving it back?"

Emily reached a hand toward him and instinct had him taking her into his arms. At least he still had one of them on his side. Lucy remained silent in the stroller and stared up at him as if assessing her own opinion.

"I'm giving it back with access to my engineer and contractor. You have an unlimited budget to do the bed-and-breakfast like you want."

Annabelle's eyes instantly filled. "Colt…but, what about your dude ranch?"

This was the tricky part. "I'm hoping I can still open it. I'm hoping we can do this together. That land can stay in your name, you can have complete control over what happens with your house, but there is something I want to merge."

Her eyes widened.

"I want you to have my name. Marry me, sweetness. Not for the land, or the house. I want your happiness and I hope that means you'll be with me and give me a second chance."

"You're serious?" she asked, blinking back tears.

"I've never been more so."

A shaky hand covered her mouth as she shook her head. Hope stilled inside him. He wanted it to grow, he wanted some sign that she was giving in.

"I want to," she whispered behind her hand. "I'm so scared."

Emily laid her head on his shoulder. Colt reached out

and wrapped an arm around Annabelle's waist, hauling her against his side.

"I'm terrified," he admitted. "This is insane for both of us, but I know what I want."

With a watery smile, she reached up and cupped the side of his face.

"The land stays in my name. I'll move in with you and let's see how things go."

Relief swept through him as he hugged her tighter against his side. "That's more than I deserve. There's one more thing."

"What's that?"

"I'd like to pay to have your father get some help. He can't do it alone."

Now she burst into tears. "You're going to take on so much with me. You must be serious if you're on board for all my baggage."

He nipped at her lips. "I'm more than on board, sweetness. I want you here more than I've ever wanted anything."

Lucy started fussing and Annabelle reached down to unfasten her. Once the baby was on Annabelle's hip, she instantly calmed.

Colt wrapped his arms around the family he'd finally found.

Annabelle smiled. "I have the perfect name you can call me."

Colt laughed. "What's that?"

"Yours."

Epilogue

Nolan hadn't had the best night at the hospital. This was the time of day when he couldn't go straight home to bed, he needed to ride to unwind.

Just as he rounded the corner to the main barn, he came up short.

Colt had his arms wrapped around Annabelle and her girls. Apparently he'd come to his senses and gone after the family he wanted.

Nolan swallowed and stepped back, so as not to be seen. He was happy for his younger brother. Nolan always figured Colt would be the first to settle down. He was a little jealous, though. Nolan would be lying to himself if he didn't admit that he wanted a family of his own. He was tired of coming home to an empty house.

When he'd built it, he'd had every intention of filling it with a wife, with children.

But he'd let that dream go. Years ago, he'd let go of the only woman he'd ever wanted. He'd hoped he'd move on and someone would come along and fill the void in his life.

As Nolan headed back to his SUV, he realized that there was only one woman he would ever care for.

Pepper Manning. He'd let her go without a fight. They'd been through hell together, but when it came to the time she needed him most, he hadn't been there. He'd messed up, but that was something he'd had to live with because there was no way to erase the past.

Living with that heartache was a battle he'd always face. He devoted his life to saving others, but he hadn't been able to save the one person he loved from heartache.

So, yeah, Nolan was jealous that his brother had found love, found a family. Because if Nolan had it to do over, he'd never let Pepper go.

But there were no second chances…right?

* * * * *

*Their weekend in Milan led to a child, but after an
accident, rich jeweler Jaeger Ballantyne can't remember
any of it! Now Piper Mills is back in his life, asking for his
help, and once again he can't resist her...*

*Read on for a sneak peek at
HIS EX'S WELL-KEPT SECRET,
the first in Joss Wood's
BALLANTYNE BILLIONAIRES series!*

She had to calm down.

She was going to see Jaeger again. Her onetime lover,
the father of her child, the man she'd spent the past eighteen
months fantasizing about. In Milan she hadn't been able to
look at him without wanting to kiss him, without wanting to
get naked with him as soon as humanly possible.

Jaeger, the same man who'd blocked her from his life.

She had to pull herself together! She was not a gauche
girl about to meet her first crush. She had sapphires to sell,
her house to save, a child to raise.

Piper turned when male voices drifted toward her, and
she immediately recognized Jaeger's deep timbre. Her skin
prickled and burned and her heart flew out of her chest.

"Miss Mills?"

His hair was slightly shorter, she noticed, his stubble a
little heavier. His eyes were still the same arresting blue, but
his shoulders seemed broader, his arms under the sleeves of
the black oxford shirt more defined. A soft leather belt was
threaded through the loops of black chinos.

The corner of his mouth tipped up, the same way it had the first time they'd met, and like before, the butterflies in her stomach crashed into one another. She couldn't, wouldn't throw herself into his arms and tell him that her mouth had missed his, that her body still craved his.

He held out his hand. "I'm Jaeger Ballantyne."

Yes, I know. We did several things to each other that, when I remember Milan, still make me blush.

What had she said in Italy? *When we meet again, we'll pretend we never saw each other naked.*

Was he really going to take her statement literally?

Jaeger shoved his hand into the pocket of his pants and rocked on his heels, his expression wary. "Okay, skipping the pleasantries. I understand you have some sapphires you'd like me to see?"

His words instantly reminded her of her mission. She'd spent one night with the Playboy of Park Avenue and he'd unknowingly given her the best gift of her life, but that wasn't why she was here. She needed him to buy the gems so she could keep her house.

Piper nodded. "Right. Yes, I have sapphires."

"I only deal in exceptional stones, Ms. Mills."

Piper reached into the side pocket of her tote bag and hauled out a knuckle-size cut sapphire. "This exceptional enough for you, Ballantyne?"

Don't miss
HIS EX'S WELL KEPT SECRET by Joss Wood,
available April 2017 wherever
Harlequin® Desire books and ebooks are sold.

And follow the rest of the Ballantynes with
REUNITED…AND PREGNANT, available June 2017,
Linc's story, available August 2017,
and Sage's story, available January 2018.

www.Harlequin.com

HDEXP0317

Whatever You're Into… Passionate Reads

Looking for more passionate reads from Harlequin®?
Fear not! Harlequin® Presents, Harlequin® Desire and
Harlequin® Blaze offer you irresistible romance stories
featuring powerful heroes.

◆HARLEQUIN *Presents*.

Do you want alpha males, decadent glamour and jet-set
lifestyles? Step into the sensational, sophisticated world of
Harlequin® Presents, where sinfully tempting heroes ignite a
fierce and wickedly irresistible passion!

◆HARLEQUIN *Desire*

Harlequin® Desire novels are powerful, passionate and
provocative contemporary romances set against a backdrop of
wealth, privilege and sweeping family saga. Alpha heroes with
a soft side meet strong-willed but vulnerable heroines amid a
dramatic world of divided loyalties, high-stakes conflict and
intense emotion.

◆HARLEQUIN *Blaze*

Harlequin® Blaze stories sizzle with strong heroines and
irresistible heroes playing the game of modern love and lust.
They're fun, sexy and always steamy.

Be sure to check out our full selection of books
within each series every month!

www.Harlequin.com

HPASSION2016

Turn your love of reading into
rewards you'll love with
Harlequin My Rewards

**Join for FREE today at
www.HarlequinMyRewards.com**

Earn **FREE BOOKS** of your choice.

Experience **EXCLUSIVE OFFERS** and contests.

Enjoy **BOOK RECOMMENDATIONS**
selected just for you.

PLUS! Sign up now
and get **500** points
right away!

Earn
FREE
REWARDS
Join
Today!
HarlequinMyRewards.com

MYR16R